The Bikini Collective

Book 1: Ocean Rules

Kate McMahon

Kate McMahon has spent the past twenty years surfing waves all over the world, and regularly arriving to events late with her hair dripping wet. After watching many of her friends compete on the world surfing tour, she wondered how she too could combine a career with her true love; her butt still hurts from pinching herself after landing the dream job as editor of *SurfGIRL* magazine in 2001. Since then, Kate has edited various preschool, tween, teen and music magazines and lives just 100 steps from the sand at Narrabeen on Sydney's Northern Beaches, where she gets up to mischief with all of her amazing surfer girlfriends.

www.katemcmahonmyword.com

 facebook.com/katemcmahonmyword

twitter.com/thekatemcmahon

 instagram.com/thebikinicollectivebook

Props to Caz, Lissie, Layne, Franziska, Morgan, Virg, Pep, Tanny, Trudy and all of my other salt-crusted surfing goddesses who share insights and stories with me between sets. Also thanks to Jenny, Gemma and Kate for their creative noggins, and my folks for raising me by the beach.

#1

Jaspa Ryder patters across her lawn and loosens the knot on top of her head, letting her sun-torched hair trickle down to her waist like a waterfall. A stray lock catches her bottom lip, and instead of brushing it away she pauses to suck on the tip, the salt dissolving on her tongue. Soon she might have to give in to her mother's pleas and wash like a regular person – you know, with soap and shampoo. But there's something about going to bed with the ocean dampening your pillow and grains of sand crusting the bed sheets that only a beach lover like her can appreciate. Besides, she's not at dire dreadlock stage yet.

Her heels bed into the blades of grass, the mildew dampening skin roughened by a predominantly bare-foot existence, while her toes burrow into the chalky sand. The first time Jaspa visited Sydney she was shocked by how different its beaches were to hers, the sand a burnt orange, heavy and coarse. Here on the north coast it's like a field of white sawdust. Jaspa pauses to watch the sun yawn its way up from the horizon, not yet ready to fully awaken. Beyond her front yard, two rabbits scurry over the carpet of bright green grass then up the hill into the thick native bush. Jaspa spent most of her childhood here playing adventure games, racing along the forested path to the top of the headland cliff. But these days, what's more important to her is what lies at the bottom, where enormous round boulders and jagged rocks spill into the ocean, swells rolling in from the Pacific surging over them and hugging the headland to produce something Jaspa dreams about every single night – Bonita Shores' best kept secret. It's Paradise Point: a wave of absolute perfection.

Tucking her surfboard under her left arm, Jaspa heads down the path to the bottom then steadies herself against the cliff face with her right hand. She waits for the set to rush at her feet before following the white-water as it crackles over the rocks back out to sea. On autopilot, she takes the easiest route out, hopping across the familiar flat boulders. She spots Mel alone in the line-up, her silhouette dancing across the shoulder-high waves, spray shooting out from beneath her feet. Jaspa paddles out to her with a grin, the ocean so still she glides over it.

'Morning,' Jaspa sings as she reaches Mel, using one hand to guide her, resting the other on the nose of her board. 'Look at that sky. We *literally* live in paradise.'

Mel slices the back of her hand through the water, sending a splash towards Jaspa. 'Ahoy, *amiga*, what took you so long?' she smirks. 'You missed our sand sesh, and I've already clocked up ten extra waves that could've been all yours.'

Jaspa shrugs. She did whack the snooze button twice this morning, favouring a few extra moments cocooned in bed rather than meeting Mel on the beach for body-weight training as she had insisted. Then there was that ten minutes Jaspa spent handwriting a note that she'll no doubt ponder and agonise over later today. But now's certainly not the time to tell Mel about that. There's no rule to say you have to share everything with your best friend, is there?

'Looks like there's plenty more left for me,' Jaspa says as a line of swell moves sluggishly towards them. 'And for him!' she giggles, pointing behind Mel as a dolphin races underwater, tailing the unbroken ride.

Jaspa strokes gracefully to greet the wave as it pitches over the sandbank. She swings under the curling lip, points the nose of her board towards the headland, leans her fingers onto the deck and glides her feet between her arms to stand tall. A startled laugh catches in her throat as the dolphin leaps from the ocean a metre away, then lands the perfect pin-drop dive.

Instead of snapping a turn into the breaking lip, Jaspa slides her front foot forward, trimming along the top of the wave, and the chase is on. A section of water swells up and Jaspa can't resist drawing on its blank canvas. Dropping down to the base of the wave, she leans so her chest almost brushes the ocean and carves her fins into the top pocket to leave a snake of whitewater. The sleek grey of the dolphin bounds in front of her like a shiny rock skimming the surface, and Jaspa wonders what it would be like to be that free. No pressures. To simply surf the waves, play with your friends, eat fish and dodge the occasional predator.

'Oh my gosh, did you see that?' Jaspa beams as she joins Mel out the back, sitting upright to straddle her board.

Mel nods excitedly. 'It was a cheeky drop-in. Every turn you did, it matched it.' Mel uses one hand to mimic Jaspa's surfing and the other as a makeshift dolphin. 'I'm sorry to say, I scored you only eight points, and your opponent a ten.'

Jaspa snorts a laugh and shakes her head. 'Trust you to turn my spiritual moment into a competition.'

'Well,' Mel says, wiggling a finger at Jaspa, 'think of it as a trial run for this weekend, and pray you don't draw a dolphin in your first heat.'

Trying not to let doubt creep in the way of her smile, Jaspa puts Mel's comment out of her mind. As if she needs reminding that the final event is two days away – the event that will supposedly decide her future as a professional surfer. She glances at Mel. Her best friend never second-guesses anything, self-confidence drips from her every pore. Just like her surfing, Mel flings herself over life's ledges and worries about the consequences later.

'Urgh, hipster alert,' Mel groans with a roll of her eyes. 'Seriously, there must be a factory somewhere manufacturing top-knots and beards. That's so 2013.'

Jaspa follows Mel's gaze back over her shoulder to see a figure paddling out from the rocks. 'Oh, I kinda like it,' she teases. 'I even had one myself this morning.' She grins, bracing for Mel's onslaught.

'Of course you did, you little hipster hippy.' Mel launches from her board onto Jaspa's. 'Here, let me help you with that,' she says, ruffling Jaspa's hair up like a bird's nest.

'Stop, stop, you've turned cray cray,' Jaspa pleads, dissolving into giggles as they both tumble into the water.

Mel tugs on her leg-rope, catapulting her board towards her, then slides onto it and strokes into a wave. 'It's time to get down to business!' she calls as she takes a freefall drop.

The ocean is calm and peaceful and Jaspa takes a moment to catch her breath, the laughter still trying to escape. Mel has been cracking her up since they were both seven years old. Even back then she had the energy of a hyperactive puppy, leading Jaspa into all sorts of mischief. There's no way she would've spray-painted Mrs Nimble's poodle, or gone doorknocking to collect for a fake charity without Mel's persuasion.

Nothing much has changed, Jaspa thinks, digging her fingernails into the wax. She's tailed her best friend into many a dull party only for Mel to instigate some crazy idea, like a handstand-off, jelly wrestling in an inflatable pool, or what the heck, it's a full moon, let's night surf! Mel manages to switch between a childlike charmer and a sassy siren who can sweet-talk her way into over-18s gigs.

Jaspa's spent almost every day with her for the past eight years, but as with any friendship, it doesn't come without friction. Most of their arguments are ignited by Mel's frustration that Jaspa doesn't think like her. If you could rip open their heads, inside Mel's you'd find a calculator, a year planner and a hammer to drive home her bluntness. Inside Jaspa's there'd be a gratitude jar, a fortune cookie and, quite possibly, dancing fairies.

'Did you see my air?' Mel sits up, pulling one knee to her chest to adjust her leg-rope.

Jaspa screws up her nose and shakes her head. 'Sorry, no, I missed it.'

'How's it goin'?' interrupts the hipster, whose top-knot is, remarkably, still dry. 'Looks fun out here.' Offering a smile from beneath his forest of chin growth, he paddles past Jaspa and sits cross-legged on his single-fin board.

'It is, we're having a ball!' Jaspa chimes as she kicks into a wave. Just as she's about to stroke into the lip she hears a 'Yo' to her left, calling her off the ride. Yanking her board back, she's stunned to see a blur of floral boardshorts fly past. She smiles and offers a 'woooo!' as the hipster weaves down the line like he's on a roller-coaster.

'Jaspa, what the hell?' Mel returns from catching a wide set, screaming over the sound of the ocean.

'Huh?' Jaspa asks with raised eyebrows, wondering if she missed another of Mel's aerials. Perhaps she should just pretend this time.

A huff shoots from Mel's chest and she shakes her head. 'Seriously, that dude just totally snaked. You were waiting first, that was *your* ride.'

'Oh.' Jaspa blinks her saucer-shaped eyes at Mel. 'I don't think he meant it. He was super friendly – I guess he just wanted a wave.'

'You let that happen to you *all* the time,' Mel growls, tightening the grip on her rail. 'Don't you get it? Guys beeline for chicks in the surf because they think we're pushovers. They assume we're at the bottom of the pecking order.'

Jaspa drops her head and fidgets with her shell neck-lace. 'Okay, okay, please don't get mad at me,' she mumbles. 'I honestly didn't think of it like that.' Jaspa glances up to see her friend's nostrils still flaring. This conversation isn't over yet.

'And anyway, you should be practising for the comp and holding your position, not letting some pony paddle to your inside.' Mel sighs and pushes the nose of her board to dive with it into the ocean. 'I'm getting the next one in. Can I still get a ride to school with you? Meet at your house?'

Jaspa nods while staring out to sea as her best friend/harshest critic milks her last wave almost to the sand. Feeling as though she and her surfing have suddenly been locked in a pressure cooker, Jaspa takes a minute to think about the note she'd been working on this morning, which now seems more important than ever. Oh crap! The note! Having your bestie live next door is convenient most of the time, except when you want to hide something from them. *I've gotta get there before Mel does,* she thinks, scrapping through the water as though being chased by a great white. There aren't many things that Jaspa hates, but confrontation is definitely one of them.

#2

'Now that's a good look, you should rock it to school next week,' Mel says, standing in the doorway of the Ryders' garden shed, her board gripped in one hand and a carrot in the other. Jaspa is wearing a bikini, still in her socks and school shoes, with her uniform hanging around her neck.

Jaspa grins at Mel then turns back to contemplate the quiver of surfboards slotted into racks along the back wall. 'I guess I got a bit excited about getting out there before it gets dark,' she says, yanking the uniform over her head and throwing it on the ground. It's not unusual for Jaspa to start one thing and be drawn into another, like a toddler distracted by shiny things. This is mostly harmless, except for moments like this morning's simultaneous grilling of banana bread, bidding on eBay for a tropical print maxi dress, and blending a smoothie. She was now the proud owner of a new frock, but it came at the expense of burnt breakfast and a kitchen splattered in milk and banana. 'Hey, you missed a couple of classes today, where were you?' Jaspa asks, trailing her finger along the surfboard rails.

Mel places her board on a strip of old carpet and crunches into the carrot. 'Tough question. Some might call it truancy, others would deem it dedication of the tallest order to my prospects as a professional surfer,' she bellows, waving her carrot to accentuate her speech.

'You skipped a school that has surfing as a subject to go surfing?' asks Jaspa, who lives out most of her rule-breaking urges vicariously through Mel, simply because the thought of disappointing her parents is too much to bear. It's not that Mel doesn't care about other people's feelings, it's just that she tends to prioritise her own.

'Your honour, I know the unreasonable nature of this notion, but in my defence it was four feet and offshore. Case closed.' Mel breaks into a giggle and slams her fist into her hand, proclaiming her innocence.

'Oi, Jaspa!' The distant voice sounds peeved, and the girls stop laughing. 'Where's the freakin' wax?'

Jaspa frowns at Mel, recognising the less than chirpy tone of her older brother. Mel rolls her eyes and mutters out of the side of her mouth, 'Brace yourself, hurricane hothead incoming.'

Tyler Tiger Ryder appears at the door with a brand

new unwaxed all-white – apart from a cluster of sponsor stickers – surfboard tucked under his arm.

'Jaspa –' he begins harshly, before softening his tone as he realises they've got company. 'Oh, hey Mel, how's it goin'?' Tyler mumbles, leaning his super-fit six-foot-two frame against the wall.

'Yo, TT, I'm good. Wanna hit the waves with us?' Mel offers, carefully pulling her brown, sun-lightened hair into a ponytail at the exact centre point of her head.

'Yeah, come and join us, Tyler, it was awesome this morning!' Jaspa agrees, keen to lighten whatever's darkening her brother's mood.

'Nah. No offence, but I've gotta train for the comp tomorrow. Don't really need a couple of chick kooks getting in my way,' he says with an arched back and a puffed-out chest. At seventeen, Tyler is blessed with the Ryder genes: tall, blond – although he might want to try a hairbrush now and again – blue-eyed, and a red-hot surfer.

For as long as Jaspa can remember, Tyler has been her hero, and he adored her too. He'd take her down to the Shores' ice-cream shop, Treat Yourself, every Friday after primary school and buy her favourite, rocky road delight, with his own pocket money. He always let her join in on his *Kelly Slater Pro Surfer* marathons when she interrupted, begging to play, even if he was on a roll of rippable proportions. Jaspa's favourite photo of Tyler shows him pushing her six-year-old self into her first wave in Bonita Bay. But lately his attitude towards her has shifted. It's like he's permanently stuck in a wetsuit two sizes too small. Uptight and agitated.

Tyler shies away from Mel's glare and goes back to interrogating Jaspa. 'I need my wax, where is it? I told you not to use it.'

Jaspa sighs deeply and looks from Mel to Tyler. 'I think I saw it in the car. Like I've said a million times, I don't use it.' She averts her eyes, keen to avoid conflict.

'Look, Mr Merry,' Mel pipes in, 'as you can clearly see, we have our own stash. But be my guest.' One hand is on her hip, the other holds out a block of pink Stick for Chicks surfboard wax. 'And I've got a pair of frilly floral halter-neck bikinis that'll top you off perfectly.' Her sarcasm is drowned out by expletives as Tyler stalks off.

'Thanks,' Jaspa says, pulling a board from the rack and wondering if she should ask Mel for a tutorial on comebacks. 'I don't know why he's always so grumpy at me lately.'

'My guess is his blue eyes are turning green at the thought of you being a kickass pro surfer. Wait, you're not taking that out are you?' Mel points to the retro round-nosed polka dot surfboard in Jaspa's hand.

'I'd planned to, it's my favourite frolicking board. Why, do you want to use it?' Jaspa offers it to Mel.

'No, it's not that … I just think you should be testing what you'll use on the weekend, don't you?'

'I guess. I hadn't really thought about it.' Jaspa sheepishly puts her beloved Dotty back into the rack.

'Don't you think you *should* be?' Mel sits on an esky and rests her elbows on her knees. 'It's like you don't even care about making the junior tour.'

Jaspa gulps. Did Mel see the note this morning? She was sure she'd got to it first, while Mel was tucking into the banana bread.

'I do, I do, I do care, I promise,' Jaspa protests, her voice pitched too high. She quickly diverts the conversation. 'What board are you taking out?'

'My five-five. Gimme your five-eight and I'll wax it up for you.' Mel gestures towards the high-performance surfboard. 'I don't mean to nag. I just can't imagine travelling to Malibu or the Maldives or anywhere else beginning with M without you.'

'I know that.' Jaspa watches Mel criss-cross the block over the board's deck. They've spent the entire year competing in junior events around Australia, and now they've finally got the chance to qualify for the world tour. No wonder Mel's pumped. It's every surfer's dream – isn't it?

'How about we practise those grab-rail tail slides?' Jaspa suggests as she steps out of her shoes and pulls off her socks.

'Yew! Sounds like a plan to me.'

They smear on sunscreen and bolt down the driveway to the beach, their leg-ropes tapping the sides of their boards with every stride.

'Damn, the swell has dropped,' Mel says as they reach the sand.

'And it's turned nor-east.' Jaspa looks towards the bay, noting the wind-affected ripples lapping the shore. 'We'll have to surf Northies.' They jog up Bonita Beach, passing old Mrs Wilson and her ancient bitsa dog out on their late afternoon stroll. The girls smile and wave, but stick to higher ground, keen to avoid any conversation that will eat into their ocean time.

Their street, Ocean View Avenue, runs the entire length of the beachfront, which they share with just ten other houses and the Shady Palm cafe, home to the scrummo Mango Magic smoothie.

'Must be cackle o'clock,' Mel says, pointing further up the beach towards the Bonita Shores Surf Life Saving Club. They can hear the chatter of middle-aged mums coming from the ocean deck, watching their children play on the grass below while debriefing on the town's goings-on. With a population of only 1800 people, everyone gets a turn at being gossip fodder.

'Promise me that's not us in thirty years,' Jaspa pleads, slowing to a walk and forming her hands into a prayer sign.

'Only if you promise me we'll never do *that* again.'

A trail of smoke drifts from the paddleboard racks underneath the club.

'Yuck. I will divorce you as a friend if you ever smoke again,' Jaspa says, screwing up her nose. Their brief stint as smokers ended when Mel's cousin Kevin caught them swiping from his pack. He promised not to snitch on the condition that they'd never spark up again. After all, he pointed out, how many world champion surfers are on the smokes?

As they near the northern headland, 900 metres from their homes, they see a light breeze blowing from the land onto the ocean, making the surface of the shoulder-high waves flawlessly smooth.

'Yes! Awesome!' Mel pumps her fist in the air. 'It's offshore and fun as!'

As weird as it may sound – except to a surfer – Northies actually faces south, meaning the ocean is calmest on a north wind. Mel and Jaspa have spent as much time learning about surfing while out of the water as they have in it: how weather patterns can affect the wave formations, the difference between rips and currents and how to get out of them safely, or use them to your advantage, and how swell and wind direction can determine the best spot to surf.

'Hey, there's Tyler.' Jaspa points towards the ocean with a forced smile.

They watch Tyler take off on his forehand on a right-hander. He wastes no time making the most of every inch the wave has to offer, jumping to his feet, driving hard into a bottom turn to face the wave, soaring fast and vertical into the top pocket of broken foam then thrusting his fins to come back down before racing to the inside section to launch sky-high, twist in mid-air and land a frontside air reverse.

'Are you kidding me? Did you see that?' Mel shoves Jaspa playfully.

'It was amazing! He's going to do seriously well tomorrow.' Jaspa's sure her brother's just antsy because of the competition. His moodiness probably has nothing to do with her at all.

Mel puts her board on the sand and clasps her hands behind her back in a stretch. 'How about we get out there and show him what these so-called chick kooks are made of?'

The identical 10-centimetre-thick tan lines around Jaspa and Mel's right ankles might make them look like a couple of weirdo one-socked tennis players to passersby. But any surfer knows this is the mark of someone who wears their leg-rope on their right foot, standing with their left foot forward, *à la* natural footers.

They strap on their leggies and wade through the shallows just as Tyler rides right up to them on his final wave, spraying them with a shore break re-entry.

'Cheers, Tyler, a shower's just what I needed,' smirks Mel. 'Nice waves, by the way.'

'Yeah, Tyler you're surfing incredible – you're definitely in form. Imagine if we all get on the tour together!' Jaspa babbles excitedly – too excitedly, judging by the look on Mel's face.

'Thanks guys, appreciate it,' he responds genuinely. 'Not qualifying is not even an option for me. It's happening. But you chicks better not get your hopes up, eh?' he belittles over his shoulder as he heads in. 'There are gonna be a lot of better surfers out there than you.'

#3

'Do you think it's true, what Tyler said?' Jaspa asks Mel as they paddle out beyond the breakers and sit upright, straddling their boards.

Mel suctions water up into her fist and squirts it towards Jaspa's face. 'Wash your mouth out, *chica*,' she demands playfully.

Jaspa's shoulders slump. She makes a whirlpool with her finger, eyes downcast. 'He's right, though. There'll be so many incredible surfers there tomorrow—'

'Who gives a crap, Jaspa?' Mel interrupts. 'We got to the final round. We deserve to be there as much as anyone else. Anyway, don't be ridic, you're more of a ripper than a pair of cut-offs.'

'Oh yeah, right.'

A wave crumbles towards them. Mel grabs the nose of her board, turning it away from Jaspa. 'Who are you, and what have you done with my eternally optimistic best friend?' she huffs, lying down and kicking furiously into the foam.

Her words ring in Jaspa's ears. Mel's right, Jaspa is always the glass-half-full girl. Or, more to the point, *who cares if it's half-full or half-empty – I know where the tap is, so why stress about it?* Jaspa remembers her tenth birthday party at Splashland water park. A black storm cloud rolled in, threatening to ruin the day, and one by one each of her friends' parents pulled the pin. Despite this, Jaspa convinced her mum to take her and Mel. How could rain possibly ruin a water park party? After hiding from the hail in the change rooms for an hour, the sky cleared, the sun shone and they practically had the place to themselves – something they didn't let the party poopers forget in a hurry.

Jaspa swooshes her legs underneath her, twirling her board in a circle. The headland looks particularly beautiful at this time of day, the setting sun casting a haze behind its smothering of trees. Savouring the slapping sound of water against fibreglass, Jaspa realises that it's these moments, not a competition vest, that make her want to be a surfer.

She glances up to see Mel paddling back in her direction. 'Jaspa! This one's yours!' Mel shouts, pointing to the set wave rolling in from the rocks.

Placing both hands on her surfboard rails, Jaspa grips tightly and swings her board around to face the shore. Lying down with her legs together and her back strong, she begins paddling into the breaking wave. She rises with the ocean as it picks her up and pitches her into a left-hander, her stomach churning with excitement. Looking over her left shoulder, she jumps to her feet, her back to the sea, and immediately carves her rail deep into the bottom of the wave and soars up, up, up, pointing the board's nose to the sky before smoothly snapping it around, leaving a 2-metre-high rooster tail of spray behind her. Lowering her centre of gravity and placing her weight on her front foot, she races the next section, ending the ride with a graceful floater, dropping tail-first and landing perfectly in the ball of foam.

Jaspa tries to mask her stoked grin as she paddles back out. It's not that she surfed it any better than usual, it's just that she's never really thought about it much before. She surfs because it's the closest thing to true love she's ever experienced, something that's always on her mind, something she can't go a day without. Up until now she's never really thought about if she's *good* at it or not. Even in competitions, it's more of a chance to fool around with friends, have the occasional day off school and perve on hot guys. Scoring prizes is the proverbial cherry. Jaspa doesn't relate to the concept of having her surfing judged and measured. What's it based on? To her, the winner is the one who's having the most fun. This weekend she'll be looking at surfing from a very different angle. Maybe it will lead to one of the biggest adventures of her life. Perhaps she does deserve to be among the best of them on the junior tour.

She sees Mel cupping her hands in front of her mouth, hooting enthusiastically. What she doesn't see is Tyler, standing 300 metres down the beach, watching her every move … with a gulp.

Swallowing his words, perhaps.

#4

Ellen Ryder has her mobile nestled between her cheek and shoulder to allow for some serious multitasking. 'Yes, of course, Tanya, it's no problem at all,' she says, pressing a herb crust onto the salmon and popping it into the oven to bake. 'Don't be silly, don't feel bad, we'll pick up Carolyn in the morning at five,' she confirms as she shuts the oven door.

Yum. The waft of roasting rosemary and sea salted sweet potato chips is far too tempting to resist. Ellen ends the call, then sneakily pinches one between her fingers, blows on it and pops it into her mouth.

'I saw that, Mum. Swipe me one too and your secret's safe with me.' Tyler enters the kitchen freshly showered and eager to relieve his post-surf starvation, willing to use bribery if necessary.

'Oh, Tyler, you scared me!' Ellen gasps, placing a

hand on her chest. 'Here. Tell no one,' she whispers dramatically as she opens the oven door. 'But be careful, they're h–'

Tyler swears through clenched teeth as the chip sizzles against his fingers, then gives his mum a playful hug before she has a chance to frown at his choice of words.

The Ryder household is pretty relaxed when it comes to the smaller, more trivial things that would raise eyebrows under a stricter watch. But respect and honesty are vital. Last year, when Tyler and two of his mates broke into the Australian Surf Museum to use their vintage mals, he demonstrated neither of these qualities, and boy did he cop the consequences. He was sentenced to cleaning the entire house, including the garden flat and the shed, banned from surfing and skateboarding for two weeks, and allowed no electronics for ten days except for the purpose of homework. But seeing the glint of disgust in his mother's eyes was the worst punishment.

'Ma, these are a-mazing. When's dinner gonna be ready?' Tyler hovers, hoping to sneak another chip.

'In about twenty minutes. Scram – go and pack for tomorrow and I'll call you when it's ready.' Ellen shoos him away with the back of her hand. 'Where's Jaspa?' she calls after him.

'Being a gumby with Mel up at Northies.'

Tyler strides upstairs to his bedroom, bitterness

swirling in his stomach. Whenever he thinks about Jaspa's surfing he is overwhelmed with irritation. It's not hate – he loves his sister. When he thinks about some of the things he says to her, imagining her friendly, carefree face staring at him, it's unbearable. How can he rile on someone so kind and nonjudgmental? Someone who unconditionally supports *his* surfing dreams? But that's exactly the problem. She's blessed with smack-into-a-pole-if-you-see-her-on-the-street beauty. She's school smart, but adorably ditsy when it comes to everyday tasks, like making toast without burning it, or not losing your phone every second day. She can have all that. *But surfing's mine*, he thinks. *I've always been the surfer. She's meant to be the tag-along.*

He slumps on the bed and stares at the walls covered in posters of surfing and bikini-clad girls from *Salt Action* magazine. Some show empty waves that he imagines himself on, deep in the blue-green barrels, or zooming down the face of a 30-foot monster, but most are of his top three heroes: John John Florence, Mick Fanning, and Tyler's main inspiration, newly-crowned 21-year-old hot shot Kazumi Hall. Kazumi is a fellow north-coast surfer who claimed the world championship during his first year on the pro tour. He's now living the life of a surfing rock star – cashed up, surfing the best waves in the world, hot chicks dripping off him ... Tyler wants that so bad it hurts. And he'll do whatever it takes to get it.

#5

Jaspa says goodbye to Mel and dawdles up the beach towards her house. She spots Tyler on the balcony outside his bedroom packing surfboards into his four-board Pro Series cover. Through the window, she can see her mother setting plates on the dining table. *Perfect timing,* she thinks, giving her a wave.

All the homes dotted along Ocean View Avenue have one thing in common – they're all designed with a beach holiday vibe. But Jaspa's is by far her favourite. Planked with a dark wood exterior and finished with an olive green tin roof and railings, it blends in perfectly with the surrounding tropical trees and plants that serve as their makeshift fence. The front of the home is panelled top to bottom in windows, a film of salt crust permanently coating them. Jaspa's ever thankful she doesn't have to live like her friend Carolyn, sardined into a two-bedroom suburban unit with her mother.

'Oh, Mum, please tell me that's salmon I can smell,' Jaspa drools as she stands dripping at the front door.

'Yes it is. It'll be ready in ten minutes, so hop upstairs for a shower and tell Dad and Tyler dinner's nearly ready.'

Jaspa patters across the open plan lounge and dining room, trying not to wet the floorboards. Her friends always rave about the stylish quirk of her house. Her dad is naturally creative, so everything he does – from presenting dinner on a plate to arranging the backyard succulents – takes on an artsy flair. Their home is decorated with unusual rustic ornaments, like an old watering can painted in a scratchy white and antique green that serves as a plant pot, or the five wooden crates that Anthony sanded back, nailed together at different angles and mounted on the wall as a bookshelf. The mountain of home decorator magazines her parents own call this style shabby chic, but Anthony labels his taste as surfside vibe.

Ellen raises an eyebrow, so Jaspa flashes her a cheeky grin. Usually she would oblige the loosely implied 'no boards in the house' rule, but tonight Jaspa needs to unscrew her fins and get prepped for the morning. Maybe.

'Hi Dad, dinner's almost ready,' she calls through

the spare room/study door before bounding up the stairs.

Eww, that's putrid. A gag heaves from Jaspa's throat as she walks into the bathroom to see the toilet seat up and the rim decorated with a few stray pubes, undies on the floor and a wet towel growing a new breed of bacteria in the bath. *Urgh. Sharing a bathroom with your feral, disgusting brother seriously sucks.* She turns on the shower and pokes her head around the door while waiting for the water to warm up.

'Tyler! You're such a messy pig! And Mum says dinner's ready.' Not bothering to wait for a reply, Jaspa steps into the shower and cranes her neck so the water runs over her face. She lathers her skyscraper legs and glides a razor over them, then pauses to think. When's she going to tell Mel – and, more importantly, *what's* she going to tell her?

'Ellen, this looks amazing. You're a keeper, all right.' Anthony gives his wife a kiss before sitting down at the table.

'Dad, are you coming to the juniors, too?' Jaspa asks, devouring some crispy salmon skin.

'Of course, button, I made sure I had the weekend off. No way I would miss seeing my two surfer stars tear it up.'

Jaspa smiles. She's thrilled both her parents are coming. Not only because she could use the moral support, and because Tyler will probably be less horrible to her with them there, but also because they're actually kinda fun. Both surf. Anthony is way better, doing top turns and getting barrels and stuff, but Ellen can ride along the wave and do little flicks that Jaspa is sure probably feel like massive carves to her mum.

Anthony works as an industrial designer for a car company. Ellen is a writer and sub-editor – Jaspa's still not quite sure what that entails exactly. Both of their offices are in Pacific Grove, the closest town, about 40 kilometres north of Bonita Shores.

Swooping in for more sweet potato chips, Jaspa slaps her forehead. 'Oops! I forgot to ring Carolyn to tell her when to be here in the morning.' She springs up to find her phone.

'Oh, don't worry, love. Tanya rang, she's been called in to work so I said we'll pick Carolyn up on the way,' Ellen replies, patting Jaspa's arm.

'Aww, thanks Mum, you're the best.'

Tyler mutters something about Pacific Grove hardly being 'on the way', then group texts his mates to see who else he can catch a ride with.

A light onshore wind squeezes in around the sliding door. Jaspa pulls the bed sheet up to her waist, doing a mental check to make sure she's packed everything she needs. Making decisions is not Jaspa's forte. Her bag is jammed with outfits to cater for all surf conditions. If it's a bigger swell she'll need more material and support to hold in her bits, so she had to pack her all-in-one tank top shorts from the retro-inspired Gidget range. But if the waves are smaller but super sucky then she'll bust out her cross-back and boy-leg bottom bikini to prevent anything popping out, up or down during freefall take-offs.

That's if she even decides to go tomorrow.

Her tummy is abuzz. Jaspa can't work out if the butterflies are dive-bombing in her stomach because she's nervous, excited, or because she's realising that maybe she doesn't actually care that much about making it through the competition. There's so much at stake for this win – a lot more than a trophy and a surf shop voucher. But is joining the tour really what she wants?

Jaspa leans over and disconnects her phone from her charger. Time to get this over with. As the butterflies grow bigger, she texts Mel.

Mel, are you awake? I've got something to tell you …
Yep, just doing a bit of ceiling staring. What's up? Don't
like the sound of this.

Please don't be mad. I'm doing my paper thing with two choices. Not sure if I want to even go in this comp or on tour.
C'mon, R U nuts?! Chuck them in the bin, you're coming. Pleeeease!
Soooooo sorry, I'm confused. You know I have to do this. Will txt l8r.

Mel doesn't reply. Jaspa takes the hand-written note from this morning out of her drawer and tears it into two pieces. Ever since she was six years old, when she couldn't decide whether her fairy doll should wear a pink or yellow tutu, Jaspa has taken to letting the universe decide. She scrawls the options on two pieces of paper, puts them in a container and pulls out one piece – and that's what she sticks to. But the older she gets, the bigger the decisions are. Like the time she had to decide whether to get a ride home from a party with 20-year-old Amanda Stone, or call her mum to pick her up like she was supposed to. Although riding with Amanda would have been way more fun, she's glad the paper ruled with her mum. Turned out Amanda had been drinking – she smashed her car into a pole. No one was badly hurt, but the incident made front-page headlines in the local paper, the *Coastal Times*.

Jaspa stares at the two choices for the twentieth time today:

Don't go in the trials. Pro-surfing pressure isn't for you, you should just be surfing for fun.

Go to the comp, surf your best and have an awesome time — you deserve to be there.

She folds the paper slips into little squares, places them inside a sock and shakes it. Her gaze drifts out the window where, through the gaps in the balcony railing, she can see the moon glistening on the ocean. She's left the curtains open so the movement of the sea, the sound of sets rolling in and whitewater foaming onto the sand can send her off to sleep. Her hand dips into the sock, fumbles about then picks out her destiny. Before she's even unravelled the message in full, she sees the last five words: *you deserve to be there.*

#6

'Speed it up, grandma,' Tyler taunts from the back of the Subaru Forester. His best mate Cooper's car was full, so a Ryder road trip it is.

'Leave her alone, don't distract her,' Ellen warns from the front passenger seat.

Jaspa had jumped at the chance to drive the 300 metres leading into the cul-de-sac. *This is what it'll be like when I turn sixteen next year,* she thinks, slipping into a daydream about the Volkswagen Beetle she so badly wants. She plans to paint daisies all over it, despite Mel's threats that there's no way in hell she'll ride in it if Jaspa does that.

Pulling into Carolyn's driveway, Jaspa's thoughts jolt back to the present as the car bumps up over the kerb, causing Anthony to wince and make a mental note to book in a wheel alignment. Jaspa waves excitedly to her friend from behind the wheel as Carolyn struggles down the driveway with a patched-up board bag and a wheelie suitcase. A white Volcom trucker cap sits high atop her short, curly black hair, and knee-length denim capris hang low on her waist underneath a baggy blue T-shirt. In their four-year friendship, Jaspa has never seen Carolyn wear a dress, but she totally rocks her beachy B-girl style.

Jaspa jumps out of the car to greet Carolyn as Anthony grabs her luggage.

'Thanks for picking me up, guys,' Carolyn says, hugging Jaspa and copping an eyeful of boob in the process. They haul the board bag on top of the other three and tie it down.

'Hey, I thought your mum was working?' Jaspa whispers, pointing at the 2001 Excel in the driveway.

'Yeah, she must've switched to the later shift.' Carolyn squares her shoulders. 'My guess is she's sleeping off the bottle of red I saw on the sink. Lucky my pay went in – she left me zero cash.'

Jaspa swings an arm around Carolyn and gives her a squeeze, not saying a word, then insists that Carolyn shotguns the window.

Arranging her legs to wedge herself into the middle seat without knocking into Tyler, Jaspa hears her phone bleep.

WELL???!!!!!

Oops. She forgot to text Mel back with the verdict.

Oh gosh sry I forgot to write back and U were already gone this morn! Yes, I'm coming, we're on our way from Carolyn's!
Lucky. I was just about to pay someone a kidnap fee to bring you here. BTW, we just passed Cooper on the highway …

Despite the air conditioner being on full blast, Jaspa feels like her body is on fire. Cooper Crawford's face flashes into her daydream like a hologram. His intense green eyes almost make Jaspa gasp aloud every time they glance her way, and his right cheek is etched with an adorable dimple. Jaspa can't pinpoint the moment when Cooper started to infiltrate her mind. Maybe it was when she was eleven, doing cartwheels in the garden, and she overheard Cooper telling Tyler his little sister was going to be hot when she was older. Or the time he helped carry her home after she stacked her skateboard at the bottom of Hill Street. Jaspa has wondered many times how the delicious warmth of Cooper's lips pressed against hers would feel. But two things would need to happen before this dream could become a reality:

1. Cooper would need to know that Jaspa exists. You know, beyond being Tyler's little sister.

2. Tyler would need to move to Siberia.

* * *

Jaspa, Carolyn and Tyler walk across the road to check in while her parents carry their luggage into their rental for the weekend.

The grassed area of the beachfront is covered in white tents and sponsor flags. Flume's 'Never Be Like You' pumps out over the loudspeaker, and the entire area is packed. Surfers wax their boards, parents and friends set up their beach blankets and gazebos, and grommets skate up and down the closed-off road. Jaspa squeezes Carolyn's shoulders in excitement. *This vibe is awesome!*

The seaside village of Wiloonga is similar to Bonita Shores, but rather than thick, tropical surroundings, green hills stretch to the horizon, hosting paddocks of cows, sheep and horses. In among the modern homes are cute fibro beach shacks of all colours, including one that's a quirky candy pink and peppermint – Jaspa's favourite so far.

The competitive hunger swirls around Jaspa as she waits at the registration desk to have her name ticked off. This is a six-star event, offering maximum point potential to add to the year's tally and a crucial springboard to qualifying for next season's World Junior Tour – the first stop on the road of professional surfing.

'Let's see who we've got,' Carolyn says, grabbing Jaspa's arm and dragging her over to the board where the heat sheets are posted. 'We're in the third round. I'm heat three, Mel six and you're in seven,' Carolyn points out, wiping her sunglasses on her T-shirt.

'How come we don't have to surf first and second rounds today?' Jaspa looks at the rows of names, wondering about the personal surfing journey of all those people. Do they love competing, or are they conflicted? Are they confident, or do they have doubts?

Tyler rolls his eyes and walks away. 'Later.'

'How could you not know that, Jaspa? We've been competing all year!' Carolyn points to the first two sheets. 'Rounds one and two are for the lower seeds, the girls we've beaten during the year or who haven't entered many of the comps.'

Jaspa nods. 'Ah, okay. So what about these spots?' she asks, tapping the two blank spaces underneath her name.

'Whoever kicks ass through round two then gets to lose against us,' Carolyn says smugly, then turns to see someone running towards them.

'My chicks!' screeches Mel, leaping between Carolyn and Jaspa, wrapping her arms around them. 'So, who are we going to beat tomorrow?'

'You two are so brutal! I've got Tara Watson,' Jaspa

says, looking at the name above hers. 'She sounds familiar, but I can't remember why.'

'She's the girl from down near Newcastle,' Mel smirks. 'You know, loves her Gosford skirts.'

'Gosford skirts?' Jaspa screws up her nose, waiting for the penny to drop.

Mel places both of her hands just below her crotch. 'Yeah, Gosford skirts – they sit just below the Entrance,' she says, straight-faced.

Carolyn snorts out a laugh, cupping her mouth and nose, and Jaspa pauses with a blank face before grabbing Mel's arm as she shakes her head.

'Oh, you're terrible! I totally know who you mean.' Jaspa remembers meeting Tara at an event on the New South Wales Central Coast in April. She was friendly enough but, in Mel's words, definitely rougher than the Tasman, and didn't mind offering her lips around to any boy who was willing.

As Mel and Carolyn continue their playful digs at Tara's expense, Jaspa moves a few steps away to look at the ocean. She just needs some time out. Surfing's not the only thing that gets judged at a contest.

'Shall we hit it for a free surf?' Mel suggests, sidling up and pointing to an empty wave down the beach.

'For sure. I can't believe no one's on it.' Jaspa nods, eager to get into the water.

Carolyn joins them, her arms folded and her hip

cocked to one side. 'Let's get out there and dominate this scene.'

'You know it,' Mel says with a determined stare, not taking her eyes off the horizon.

Jaspa glances between Mel and Carolyn and wonders how she's going to fit into this picture.

Let the games begin.

#7

Downward dog, high plank into cobra, repeat. Jaspa is on the beach with Mel and Carolyn, smashing out some yoga stretches as they warm up for their practice heat. Hearing several wolf whistles behind them, they are mortified to see six surfer guys walking past, admiring the girls' unintentionally crowd-pleasing butt thrusts.

'Oh my god, I think that's Matt Thompson and the WA team,' Mel says as the three girls abruptly sit on the sand to put on their leg-ropes, ending the peep show.

'Well, ten bucks says they aren't whistling at these tree stumps,' Carolyn laughs, slapping her thighs.

'Stop that, you.' Jaspa pokes at Carolyn's butt cheek through her sporty two-piece. 'I'd kill to have your toned legs – you can probably top turn better than they can.'

Mel stands up with her board tucked under her arm

and the slack of her leg-rope looped over her fingers, coaxing the two girls to their feet. 'Right, down to business,' she says, looking out to sea. 'Twenty minute heat, best three waves, we judge each other.'

Jaspa bites her bottom lip as she sees Mel and Carolyn set their stopwatches. 'I, err, I forgot to bring my watch,' she shrugs.

'We can give you time calls for this practice, but you'll need one for the comp,' Mel calls over her shoulder, then launches into the ocean ahead of the girls.

'Too easy, I'll just borrow Dad's,' Jaspa says to Carolyn as they paddle out at the open beach break, duckdiving under the head-high waves that slam onto a shallow sand bank.

Jaspa strokes into a wave but quickly pulls back her board to avoid getting dumped. 'Whoa, it's a bit sucky and straight.'

Mel froths about, trying to find the best place to sit. 'There are some longer rides, you just have to choose the right one.'

Carolyn paddles strongly past Jaspa for a late take-off, dropping on her forehand into a hollow left. She freefalls with the lip of the wave and just as it looks like she's going to eat it, Carolyn lands with a thump, tucks tightly into a closeout barrel and then punches through the back of the wave, still standing on her board.

'I thought you were about to get seriously sand

crumbed!' screams Jaspa, impressed by her friend's quick exit.

'Nice save,' Mel offers. 'I give you a 2.5.'

Had the wave opened up for Carolyn to ride right through the thick tube, it would've been a perfect ten.

Mel powers towards a line of swell swooping in from the south and strokes into a right-hander. She pops to her feet, facing the ocean, and waits until she's at the base of the wave to carve her rail through the water and lean the full weight of her body into a bottom turn. Then, angling the nose of her board up towards the breaking section of the wave, Mel uses her back foot to thrust her fins into the air and whip the board back around underneath her. She links two more turns before straightening out as the wave shuts down in front of her.

'That could be a heat winner,' Carolyn shouts as Mel makes her way back out to them. 'An 8.5 for you.'

'Oh, man, that was a fun little runner.' Mel sits up on her board. 'I blew it, though. I should've ollied to get more air into the first turn.'

'It looked amazing from where we were sitting,' Jaspa says, fascinated at how surfers can have such different styles but be equally incredible. Mel is zippy and light, and is already starting to land aerials. But Jaspa also admires the power in Carolyn's turns – the amount of spray she produces could fill a swimming pool. Jaspa's eager to get her first wave, turning to catch what looks to be another right-hander. She springs to her feet and snaps a smooth and explosive manoeuvre into the wave's top pocket, but it doesn't offer any more face to ride along, so Jaspa swan dives over the back of the sandy foam.

'The ride was short, but we'll give you a four for the sick turn,' Mel says. 'And a ten for the dismount!'

The three friends finish their twenty-minute mock heat, going wave for wave. Mel is unanimously deemed the winner, and Jaspa's reminded that wave choice in less-than-perfect conditions is what will give them the edge over their competitors tomorrow. *Tomorrow.* Jaspa's belly suddenly bubbles with nerves.

'Shhh, can you hear that?' Jaspa whispers, pausing at the shore to listen to the announcement over the loud speaker.

'Next in the water we have Michael Trimm from Manly, Snapper Rocks' Sean Blake, Tyler Ryder of Bonita Shores and Todd Grainger from Middleton,' blares the commentator.

'Oh phew, we didn't miss Tyler's heat.' Jaspa coaxes Mel and Carolyn towards the tent her parents are sitting under. Anthony throws each of the girls an apple as they stand their boards upright, wedging the noses into the sand, and find a spare bit of picnic rug to plonk down onto.

'How's Tyler doing?' Jaspa asks, sinking her teeth into the apple and sucking up the juice dripping down from her mouth.

'Is he cool, calm and collected as usual?' Mel adds with a fair serving of sarcasm.

Jaspa snuffles back a laugh at Mel's bluntness. She'd love to tell Tyler to chillax, but that'd be harder for him to swallow than a clump of seaweed.

'He's not too bad, actually,' Ellen says with a bit of maternal diplomacy.

'This should be a fairly easy heat for him,' Anthony adds. 'It's the next few he'll have to focus on. If he wants to make the world juniors, he needs to reach the semi-finals.'

'Hey, me too,' Carolyn says, swinging around to face Anthony and lifting her cap from over her eyes.

This contest is the highest ranked of the entire amateur Australian Junior Tour, and rewards with maximum point potential. Jaspa ponders the logistics. 'So, how many get to travel next year?' she asks Mel while digging her coral-pink painted toes into the sand.

'Aussies? Eight girls and thirteen guys. It's different for each country.' Mel looks at Jaspa then at Carolyn, and then stares out to sea. 'I wonder who the other five joining us will be.'

Anthony scribbles notes on his printed heat sheets, reminiscent of his days as head judge for the local boardriders. 'What about you, Mel?' he asks, writing down the score of Tyler's last ride. 'What do you need to qualify?'

She holds three fingers above her head without turning around. 'But I'm aiming for second.'

Jaspa breathes a quiet sigh of relief, thankful for a subject change as she sees her brother jog from the water to return his rash vest. His score of 17.8 left his challengers in a combination situation – where they needed a further two waves to beat him. Even from a distance she can see a massive smile on his face. Phew – he might be just bearable for the next twenty-four hours. Jaspa stays silent, preferring not to involve herself in the discussion of points and qualifying that continues around her. She's aware that the only reason Mel didn't say 'first' is because that's exactly what Jaspa needs to come to qualify for the junior tour. And that seems like a ridiculous notion.

#8

Mel pushes through the gate into the courtyard to see Carolyn sitting at the outdoor bamboo setting flicking through a copy of Tyler's *Salt Action* magazine. 'This is such crap!' Carolyn mutters through gritted teeth.

'Oooh, someone's fired up.' Mel pokes at Carolyn's shoulders, then swings into the seat next to her. She loves it when other people are as dramatic as she is – some call it psychopathic, she calls it passionate.

Jaspa appears at the sliding door with two glasses of watermelon and mint juice. 'Mum, we'll need another one. Mel's here,' she calls over her shoulder, offering a drink to each of her friends.

'Check this.' Carolyn turns aggressively from page to page. 'The only pics of girls in this mag are those posing in g-bangers.'

'And who are definitely *not* on a surfboard,' Mel adds.

Jaspa leans back and rests her foot on Mel's seat. 'Did you notice the only mention of girls' surfing is a paragraph in the news section about Trudy Hardwick winning her *third* world title. A *paragraph!*' It's only recently Jaspa has realised how absurd something like this is. She's always subconsciously accepted not seeing females represented in sport as much as men – she just got used to it. And besides, what could she do about it anyway?

'Oh, what have we here, then?' Mel holds out her phone to add fire to the topic. 'Their website has a "chicks" tab, so let's see ...'

Carolyn snatches the phone in anticipation of what lies a click away. 'Oh, this is such BS!' she shouts, throwing the phone back at Mel in disgust.

Jaspa shuffles in close as Mel scrolls through endless self-submitted images of wannabe swimwear models with their ridiculously stupid duck-pouts and flared nostrils, kneeling in the sand. Oh, and they're dripping wet from the ocean. Of course. Mustn't forget about the ocean – it's a surfing mag, after all.

Then there are their equally ridiculous bios:

Name: Tammy Delicious
Age: 18
From: Currumbin, Qld

Likes: Energetic surfer boys who can kiss all night
Dislikes: Clothing
Skill: Getting any guy I want, even yours

Mel sticks her index finger down her throat and gags. 'Why would you put girls in bikinis doing *nothing* in the mag when you could easily put girls *surfing*?'

'Exactly,' Jaspa agrees, tugging the strap of her swimmers. 'We wear bikinis and we're not bimbos.'

Carolyn slumps back in her chair with an exhausted sigh. 'It's not gonna change, though. There's nothing we can do about it.'

Jaspa nods. There's no way three teenagers from a small town can possibly make a difference.

Mel narrows her eyes and slams her palms on the table. 'Maybe there is ... Jazz, grab your laptop.' She grins smugly and wriggles her fingers in the air like a villain in a Disney film. 'We, my shredding sistas, are writing a letter to the editor.'

Dear Salt Action,

We're writing to commend you on all of your amazing, exhilarating surf imagery and articles, capturing the essence of everything we love about surfing: the waves, the locations, the hardware, the stories, the manoeuvres. However, there's one question burning our salt-crusted lips: where are the female surfers? In your latest edition there's only one paragraph dedicated to Trudy Hard-

wick's third world title win – and she's Australian, and lives in the same town your magazine is published in! Are there any other images of surfing females to be found between page one and 138? Nup. Nope. A big fat NO! Yet page after page is littered with horrid skanks for you to perve on. Sexist pigs!

Mel stops typing. 'It needs more. What else do we want to say?'

'Does it sound a little harsh?' Jaspa asks, screwing up her nose.

'No … yes. It's *supposed* to sound harsh. It's freakin' outrageous!'

'Yeah, true. But perhaps we need to explain *why*?'

'Dude, she did explain why,' Carolyn jumps in, scraping her finger around the rim of her glass and licking off remnants of juice. 'Because they're sexist!'

Jaspa's eyes dart between them. She sighs, remembering her mum's advice when Maxine Margsworth tormented her throughout the whole of year eight. If she wasn't posting pictures online of Jaspa's head pasted on the bodies of giraffes, she was spreading lies that Jaspa wore her mother's underwear.

Nothing she tried worked, until one day Jaspa's mother suggested she talk it out with Maxine and tell her *why* her actions were hurting her; that for the first time in her life she couldn't be herself and how unfair that was. And it worked. Not only did Maxine quit harassing Jaspa, but through a spill of built-up tears she confessed her desire to form true friendships rather than those based on being bitchy. That's not to say Jaspa and Maxine then became besties, but at least Maxine stopped hassling her.

Jaspa shuffles in her seat and leans forward. 'Look, I just don't think we should say that stuff about other girls – at least not in that way. It's a bit mean. And I don't think being on the attack helps, either. What's the real reason we want them to cover female surfing?'

'Ah, the voice of reason, she speaks. You're right, you're totally right. How about …' Mel deletes a line of text and starts typing.

A big fat NO! Yet, page after page is littered with scantily clad girls purely for your perving pleasure. This reeks of sexism. We've got nothing against the female form or girls in swimwear, because – stop the press – we wear bikinis, too. And rashies and wetties. What we want is to be inspired by amazing, powerful, courageous, talented women surfing waves. Isn't this the kind of role model you'd prefer for your sisters, nieces, daughters …? You're in a position where you can inspire surfers, and we sure hope that includes us.
Yours sincerely in surfing,
Mel, Jaspa and Carolyn – The Bikini Collective
Bonita Shores, NSW

Mel sits upright in her chair with an expression of cheeky satisfaction on her face.

'Ha, The Bikini Collective, you're a genius!' Jaspa giggles, reading over Mel's shoulder. 'It's like you're giving power back to the word "bikini", associating it with action instead of posing. I love it!'

'Exactly, that's a sick analogy! It's like that Pussy Riot band, remember them?'

Carolyn flicks her fingers together. 'Weren't they those Russian punk chicks?'

'Yep, that's them. They took the word "pussy", which can be degrading, and turned it badass. We can do the same.' Mel looks at Carolyn with a wide grin. 'Are you cool with that? It sounds catchy, and I didn't want those other girls giving our favourite attire a bad name.'

Carolyn shrugs her shoulders. 'Yeah, sure. I mean, I wear 'em so why not? And The Wetsuit Collective doesn't sound nearly as good.'

Mel nods, types in *letters@saltactionmag.com* and presses send.

'Ooh, I wonder if they'll publish it?' squeals Jaspa.

'They won't have any choice. Watch this.' Mel presses select-all and copy, then opens Facebook and pastes their letter on *Salt Action*'s profile page.

'Sharing is caring!'

#9

Jaspa picks up the pace to join her two jogging buddies, who are at least 10 metres in front. She may have the advantage of long legs, but Mel and Carolyn definitely invest a lot more time in their fitness than Jaspa does. In fact, she hates running; it hurts her boobs and seems pointless unless you actually have somewhere to be. Like the corner store for treats, for instance.

Their feet pound on the chalk-white sand, forming a rhythmic pattern in time with the dance track they've synchronised between all three phones.

'Ugh, the torture's nearly over,' Jaspa pants from behind, relieved to see the dots of colour in the distance beginning to form the shape of tents and beachgoers as they get closer.

'Jaspa, you need to push yourself harder and tap

into your inner endorphins. It's a buzz,' Mel says through steady breaths.

Jaspa glances at her with a crease of doubt at the centre of her brow and licks sweat from her lips.

'She's right, Jaspa,' Carolyn joins in, removing one earphone. 'Cardio will really help you with your paddle-outs and surf stamina. Embrace it!'

Jaspa groans. *The only thing I want to embrace is a big veggie burger and perhaps a yummy boy.* Each time she tries to slow her pace Mel and Carolyn grab an arm each and pull her along, like two monkeys leading a reluctant emu.

Their training session ends at the drinking fountain, where Jaspa clasps her hands on her knees and takes a moment to steady her breathing.

'What's the deal over there?' Mel wonders, pointing towards a crowd of people encircling a fenced-off grassy area behind the tents. As they wander over, they hear boisterous cheers, followed by gasps. A voice bellows enthusiastically over a speaker.

'Can he beat the record of forty-six seconds? Oh, he's just come unstuck, what a bummer!'

Peering over the crowd, Jaspa sees a boy tumbling off a mechanical surfboard covered in Rocket Fuel stickers, the latest energy drink to launch itself onto the surfing scene.

'Oh cool, it's a motorised surfboard thingy,' she says

to Mel and Carolyn, who drop down from their tippy toes.

'Do we have any more takers?' shrieks the commentator, far too excitedly. 'Come around the side and put your name down. You could win yourself some sick prizes!'

Mel grabs her two friends by the arm and drags them towards the registration area before they have a chance to protest.

'Hey, girls, are you keen on entering?' asks a guy from behind the desk. All three of them stop and stare.

For starters, he's shirtless, exposing his dark, freckle-free skin and a tattoo of a wave and sunrise inked on his left inner bicep. Sticking out from under his Rocket Fuel cap are tufts of brown wavy hair with sun-bleached tips, and his grey eyes look like a puddle of ash. Jaspa notices that his gaze is fixed in Mel's direction, rendering her speechless. Jaspa's equally silent. She's too busy, keeping one eye on this spectacular looking guy and the other on Mel, struggling to believe her best friend has been muted.

Carolyn pipes up, martyring herself as the icebreaker. It's rare she's dumbstruck by dudes, as they usually end up in the friend zone.

'Yep, count us in, where do we sign up?'

He holds his gaze on Mel a moment longer, long enough to make her grin, then turns to Carolyn with a friendly smile and hands her a pen and a form.

'Just chuck your names on there and you'll be up in about five. Have you done this before?'

'Yeah, err, I mean no. I mean …'

Jaspa swallows back a laugh. *Whoa, this guy's good; he even makes Carolyn stumble.*

'Well, we all surf, but not mechanically.' Carolyn writes down their names and then they retreat to debrief on exactly what just happened.

'He was *so* checking you out, Mel. Who is he?' Carolyn asks once they're out of earshot.

'That's Kazumi Hall,' Jaspa whispers. 'Tyler has posters of him all over his wall.'

'Oh, right, it is, too,' Carolyn nods. 'He looks different with dry hair.'

Mel glances back at Kazumi only to catch him gawking straight at her. Instead of shying away, she removes her sunglasses, narrows her eyes, tilts her mouth in a half smile and raises one eyebrow.

'Oh my god, you're giving him the hook-up look!' Jaspa says, poking Mel in the ribs. 'I haven't seen that since Anna Roland's party when you seduced, what was it, like, ten guys?'

'I think it was twenty,' Carolyn says with a semi-straight face.

'It was two, you bitches,' Mel laughs, 'so shut up! It was just one of life's little slip ups.'

'More like slip *in* – of the tongue,' Carolyn teases, jumping back before Mel can tackle her.

'Hey!' interrupts a voice behind them. 'This is for you from Kazumi.' A micro grommet, who is no more than eight years old, wearing skinny jeans and an over-sized fedora holds out a piece of paper for Mel.

'Oh, thanks little dude,' she says in surprise, and starts to unfold it. Jaspa and Carolyn look over her shoulder to read:

Hey, comp closing party tomorrow night at the Rocket Fuel house, 7 Whaler Road, you're all invited. Hope to see you there. Yo, KH

'Ooh, looks like you're in for another slip up, Mel,' Carolyn jokes.

Jaspa silences them with her hand. 'Mel, you're up, they just called your name. Go, go!' She catches the phone Mel tosses her and admires her friend's confident strut. If anyone has the mindset to be a world champion surfer one day, surely it's Mel. Jaspa watches her kick off her thongs underneath a box covered in a thick blue waterproof cover, pump her fist at the sea of people and climb on top of the 6-foot-long board. Jaspa hopes *she* doesn't have to make such a dramatic entrance.

'Get up there, Mel, and show us your moves!' pumps the commentator.

Mel decides to try something different and lies down on the board, pretending to paddle.

'Look, ladies and gentlemen, she's seen a wave she wants!'

The crowd shouts encouragement as the board

starts rocking from side to side and Mel pops to her feet. However, just as she's about to land, the board changes direction, pivoting from nose to tail. The transition takes her by surprise and with too much weight on her front foot, she topples forward and hits the grass in a running motion.

'Oh no, we've got a wipeout! I'm sorry, Mel, but that was only a ten-second session. Next we've got Jaspa. Come on up, surfer girl!'

'It's really hard,' Mel says as she passes Jaspa. 'Don't try and be a smartarse like I did, just hang on!' They high-five each other and Jaspa climbs onto the board.

The Beach Boys' 'Surfin' USA' starts playing and the crowd hoots. Jaspa feels the board start to rock from side to side and then seesaw up and down. She's concentrating so hard she forgets there are more than fifty pairs of eyeballs on her. The board swings around 180 degrees clockwise, so she crouches down low and rides through the manoeuvre, hearing the crowd start to count, '… twenty-five, twenty-six, twenty-seven …'

The commentator announces that they're going to crank things up a notch. The mechanical board swings ninety degrees clockwise, so Jaspa dips her front shoulder for stability and flows with the movement. On the way around she catches a glimpse of Tyler, who's giving her the filthy look usually reserved for the most blatant of wave drop-in perpetrators. What has she done now? She's barely seen him all day! Maybe she used too much of the sunscreen? Or maybe that was his pawpaw she scoffed this morning? Oh god, maybe he's picked up on her Cooper crush? *Nooooo!* Her thoughts travel one way while the board swings the other, sending her bum-first onto the grass.

'Jaspa Ryder takes a tumble, folks, just shy of thirty-eight seconds,' the commentator announces. 'Have we got Carolyn here?'

Mel stretches up her arm and points at Carolyn. 'She's here! Our only hope left is here!' She gives Carolyn a playful push towards the limelight.

'Yeah, Carolyn!' encourages Jaspa, as she dusts the grass from her butt and joins Mel, eager to get her take on what's behind Tyler's death stares.

'Whoa, look at Carolyn, she's absolutely dominating.' Jaspa links arms with Mel and they watch their friend intently. Carolyn's low centre of gravity and ability to flex her ankles for prompt weight shift make her more than a match for the board's movements. The controller rolls her back, forth, sideways, and even throws in a spiralling 360-degree backhand turn, and she rides through each manoeuvre without a wobble or flail to be seen. A cluster of year eight surfers, who hang out at the surf shop she works in, go totally nuts with screams of 'yew!'. Carolyn not only beats the record but smashes it, staying on for one minute and eight seconds. She scores a GoPro Hero3+ and a $100 voucher for the local pizza place.

'This is so sick, we can make mini surf movies,' Carolyn says, admiring her prize. There's no way she could ever afford such gadgetry.

'Excuse me, can I get a quick photo for our website?' asks a guy decked head-to-toe in Rocket Fuel gear.

'Sure can,' Carolyn replies, still buzzing from her victory. She holds up her prizes and gives the camera her best almighty attitude-ridden smeer – half smile, half sneer.

'Hey girls, quick, quick, let's go,' Jaspa pleads, spotting Tyler and Cooper walking towards them – and doing an awful job of pretending not to notice.

'Nice one, Jaspa. I can't believe you idiots did that!' Tyler spews.

'What, why shouldn't we?' Jaspa replies with a combination of annoyance and confusion. How is entering a mechanical surfboard comp any of her big brother's business? She sees Mel open her mouth, probably about to tell Tyler to rack off, but he cuts her off.

'Good on ya, write to the mag with that ranting femmo letter.' Tyler was mortified. All his friends had read it and commented on it.

'Wait, how do you know ...' Jaspa begins, before remembering the Facebook post. Jaspa shoots her friends a look to suggest they should exit stage left immediately, and get their phones into their hands, *pronto*.

#10

Two thousand likes, ninety-three shares and 202 comments from all over the world.

'Check this one out,' Mel says, scrolling down her screen, stopping at a profile picture of a girl standing at the Hollywood sign with a surfboard. 'Wow, I wonder if she's actually from California? "Way to go, girls! Good on you for speaking up and saying what we're all thinking. Surfer girls deserve to get exposure, too, it's the only way the sport will grow!"'

'Oh, this one doesn't sound happy.' Jaspa points to a new post from a guy called Sanga, whose profile picture shows him with temporary tattoos of the Australian flag all over his face. 'Eww, he's awful. Get this: "Rack off ya butch bitches, we want tits and ass, the more flesh the better!"' Jaspa cringes, wondering how people like that can exist in the world. He could be someone's brother or even boyfriend. Yuck.

'Yeah, there are a few weirdos,' Mel says, speed-reading. 'But most of it is pretty positive, even from the guys.'

'Jaspa?' Jaspa looks up as she hears her mum calling from downstairs.

Footsteps approach. 'Jaspa, can I come in?' Ellen asks, pushing open the bedroom door.

'Yeah, Mum. What's up?' The phone continuously beeps in Jaspa's hand with notifications.

'The *Coastal Times* called to say they wanted to speak to you three – something about a letter?' Ellen has free-lanced for the *Times* for years.

'What, are you serious?' Mel screams, startling Ellen. 'What did they say? Tell us everything!' She bounces on the bed on her knees. Jaspa shuffles closer to Carolyn, making room for Mel's enthusiasm.

'They just wanted to know if they could interview you. So, what letter are they talking about?' Ellen leans against the door and folds her arms with a hint of suspicion.

'This, look,' Jaspa says, handing her phone to her mother. 'We're sick of *Salt Action* being so sexist, so Mel wrote a letter.'

Mel waits a moment for Jaspa to elaborate, then jumps in. 'Make sure you read the post *and* the comments.'

Ellen stares intently at the screen, reading, then looks up at them. 'Good for you, girls. It's articulate, maturely written, to the point and obviously a fair assumption, judging by the response it's getting.'

Jaspa smiles at Carolyn, knowing neither of them would ever have had the initiative to speak out like this. Banging your fist down on a table with your two best friends is very different to sticking up your middle finger in a public arena. Mel has always had a way of forcing Jaspa outside of her social comfort zone before she even realises she's in one.

In their first year of high school they saw four year twelve girls leave a pile of empty cans and chip packets on the beach. Before she knew it, Jaspa was following Mel, each with a pile of the rubbish in their arms, to the litterers' open car windows. They threw the waste into the girls' laps, asking if they'd forgotten something.

Then they hid in the dunes for an hour while the black souped-up Commodore cruised the streets in search of them. Was it worth the risk of their DNA ending up under the nails of some inner west scrappers? Heck yeah. Would she have done it without Mel's instigation? Heck no.

Mel takes back her phone to enter the number of the *Coastal Times* journalist into her contacts. Jaspa sees the familiar look in Mel's eyes. We're in this together, she realises. No backing down now.

'Her name's Josephine Brown and she's expecting

your call,' Ellen says, masking her pride under a subtle smile. She glances at her watch. 'I'll run out and get some groceries for tonight. What would you like for dinner?' she asks. Jaspa cocks her head and bites down on her bottom lip, trying to prompt culinary inspiration. Carolyn suddenly sits upright and whacks Jaspa's thigh with the back of her hand.

'Hey, let's use the pizza voucher I won. It's for a hundred bucks, so you should all come, you too Mel.' Carolyn seems to be bubbling with empowerment. After all those years of having to rely on Jaspa's generosity, sharing her lunch whenever Carolyn's mum forgot to put 'feed child' on her to-do list, she's sure Carolyn feels like she's repaying the favour.

Jaspa catches Carolyn's hand. 'Yes, what an awesome idea!' she beams.

Mel interrupts, holding her phone in the air. 'Righto, who's going to call this Josephine, then?'

Jaspa and Carolyn smirk at each other and simultaneously blurt out a single laugh. 'Who do you think?'

Needing no further encouragement, Mel presses the saved number and puts her phone on speaker. After five rings, someone answers.

'Josephine Brown speaking,' chimes a women's low-toned, husky voice – the kind you hear reading the triple j news. Mel draws in a breath, realising she hasn't really thought about what to say.

'Oh, hi, this is Melissa Appleby here ... we're

returning your call regarding the letter to *Salt Action* mag.' Mel motions for the girls to be silent as they wait for a response, staring intently at the phone.

'Thank you for calling me back, Melissa. The *Coastal Times* would like to run an article on the letter you and your friends wrote to the magazine, and wondered if you'd be available for an interview?'

Mel raises her eyebrows at her friends, who nod their approval, then leans towards the phone. 'Yes, we'd love to be involved. But we're down the coast for a comp until Sunday.'

'If possible, I'd like to speak to you this afternoon – I'm already in Wiloonga covering the junior event. We're hoping to run the story in Monday's paper.' Mel asks Josephine to hold for a moment, then mutes the phone and turns to her friends.

'What do you think? It'll eat into our afternoon surf session, and we should be training for the comp, but …'

'We should do it, it's for the good of girls' surfing,' Carolyn leaps in.

Jaspa nods rapidly and laughs at Mel's attempt at trying to keep cool. 'Of course we're doing it! It'll be heaps of fun.'

Mel unmutes the phone and brings it up to her ear. 'Hi, sorry to keep you. We'd love to do the interview.' She pauses, listening. 'Oh wow, sure! Three pm? Great, see you then.' Mel chucks the phone on the bed and starts dancing around the room. 'You're not going to believe this,' she sings.

'What, what, what, tell us!' Jaspa pleads as Mel playfully pinches her cheeks.

'We, my fine surfer friends, have also been asked to do a photo shoot!'

Jaspa flops on the bed with a wide grin. This is totally worth any grief her brother can dish out. I mean, come on … a photo shoot? Another scoop of awesome added to an already awesome day of AWESOMENESS.

#11

Cooper approaches the counter of Bite Size, Wiloonga's only cafe, and hands over his vibrating beeper. A waitress wearing a scoop-neck white T-shirt, her auburn hair styled back into a plait, brings two plates over to Cooper and picks up the beeper, which is still buzzing. 'We could have some fun later, me and you,' she suggests, leaning on her forearms. Cooper blurts out a guffaw, which isn't exactly the smooth and suggestive response he was baited for.

'Yeah, maybe,' is all he can offer, picking up the plates. 'Thanks, looks delicious,' he adds, gesturing towards the grilled fish burgers and beer-battered chips.

'Yep, it sure does,' the waitress flirts back with a grin, her eyes fixed on Cooper, with no interest whatsoever in his lunch. Oblivious, Cooper lets the scoring potential pass when the girl looks past his shoulder to her next target. 'Hey handsome, what can I get ya … besides me?'

When a surf comp's in town, and surfers get hungry, and you work in the only cafe in town, it's like a smorgasbord of yummy boys.

Cooper sits on the tree stump stool opposite Tyler in the cafe's courtyard. Tyler wraps both hands around his burger, squashes it and then hoovers at least a third of the meal in one bite. 'She's pretty hot,' he mumbles, mayonnaise dripping down onto his bare belly.

Shoving a few fries into his mouth, Cooper looks over his shoulder at the waitress, who's now perched on the lap of Cooper's successor. 'Yeah, kinda,' he shrugs, not too cut about the boat he just missed.

Tyler looks over the top of his burger at the waitress, who's giggling as she attempts to suck a strawberry thickshake up through a straw. Tyler knows she's not really Cooper's type. Most of Cooper's girlfriends have a splash of sweet in their DNA. If wild is on the menu, it's rare that Cooper will order it. Tyler, on the other hand …

Cooper's first serious hook-up was with Tiffany Stevens, the girl he'd been dating since year nine when, after waiting for almost two years, they finally took the plunge on her sixteenth birthday. While her parents were up the coast visiting relatives, she filled her room with sandalwood-scented candles, put on Angus and Julia Stone and they had a night they'd remember forever, even though they broke up five months later.

Tyler's, by comparison, was at an end-of-year-ten garage party with a year twelve seductress who may have been called Bronwyn – too wasted to recall the finer details.

'Dude, you could score so many more chicks by using those pretty-boy looks for evil instead of good,' Tyler teases with a grin. A girl could throw herself at Cooper's feet and he'd probably think she'd simply dropped something.

'Well, seeing as you brought it up ...' Cooper wipes the remnants of smeared tomato sauce off his plate with his last hot chip and stuffs it in his mouth. 'Look, the thing is, I think I like ...' he begins, ready to spill the thing that's been on his mind for months now. But before he can finish, a roll of board tape flies through the air and lands on their table, knocking over the salt shaker.

'Hey, Ryder, use that to muzzle ya stupid sister and her friends,' riles Andrew Olsen, a bruiser from Maroubra. A Southern Cross tattoo is spread across his pecs, which bulge from beneath a navy blue tank top. 'As if we need girls surfing in magazines when we can perve at 'em gettin' their titties out!' He cups his hands underneath his chest and jiggles to illustrate his point.

'Rack off, Olsen,' Tyler retaliates, rising from his stool and letting it tip over. 'Go near my sister and I'll smash you from here back to the southern hovel you came from.' Tyler is furious about Jaspa's public rant – it's causing him major embarrassment. He can't believe she would do this to him.

'I'd much rather have more chicks in the line-up than have to look at ugly mugs like you,' Cooper humours, trying to lighten the debate and encouraging Tyler to sit back down. Andrew's a known hothead, and Cooper's seen his fists in action before. That's not something they should be provoking.

A group of three girls seated a few tables away listen in on the argument. The blonde turns to her friends with a quizzical look.

'What are they talking about?'

Her friend Pepita, her black hair blunted at the fringe and folding into a shoulder-length bob, whacks the side of her head for dramatic effect. 'I forgot to tell you,' she says, beckoning them closer. 'That Jaspa chick and her friends wrote a letter on *Salt Action*'s Facebook page, grilling them about not featuring any girls surfing in the mag.'

'Oh my god, that's awesome. About time,' says the third girl, lightly clapping her hands. Pepita brings up the post on her phone and the three of them scroll through, reading the comments aloud with every intention of being heard.

Andrew and his hometown mates cough an

unsubtle 'shut up' into their hands, projected in the girls' direction.

Pepita continues to read the posts, brushing aside the flying remarks until one word hits a nerve: *kooks*. She springs up and walks with purpose over to Andrew's table. Standing at just five foot two, it's like a Jack Russell confronting a pack of Rottweilers.

Pepita prides herself on her koala-like calm, which she gets from her Australian father, and the snake-like strike she gets from her Malaysian mother.

Tyler and Cooper watch the girl with dark hair approaching the table of brutes. 'You ready to back me up if things turn ugly?' Cooper asks.

Tyler shoots Cooper a look to suggest he's gotta be kidding. 'Oh, you're *not* kidding, are you?' He slumps on his stool with an annoyed groan. Since when did he sign up for feminist fight club? 'Urgh. Okay, yeah, I guess.'

'How dare you call us kooks? You have no idea what you're talking about!' Pepita snaps, pointing her OPI Big Red Apple-polished finger towards the group of guys.

'You're a girl surfer, the lesser breed, honey. Get used to it,' snubs one of Andrew's sidekicks, as his friends snicker in support.

Pepita's face tightens and her breath catches in her throat. No way is she letting this go. 'You ignorant loser. If you took the time to watch girls surfing, you might learn a thing or two about style!'

'The only style I give a rats about is when you duck-dive in front of me, sweetheart,' Andrew drawls with a sleazy curl of his upper lip.

Pepita calmly picks up the jug of water in front of her and splashes its contents all over Andrew's face. 'There, you putrid excuse of a human!' she spits, slamming it back down on the table. 'Next time I spray you like that, it'll be with my board. Now show some respect!'

Stunned by a cocktail of awe and astonishment, her two friends collect their jaws off the floor and pull Pepita away from any potential payback. As Tyler and Cooper slip out through the back door, they hear the cafe rumble behind them as the king of Maroubra drowns in the laughter erupting around the room, every drop at his expense.

#12

'Yes, definitely those ones. The colour suits you and they sit nice on your hips,' Jaspa offers around the door, hoping to quash Carolyn's self-doubt.

Carolyn studies herself in the mirror, donning brown and blue tie-dyed swimmers, and decides to take Jaspa's word for it. 'Well, there's nothin' I can do about my friend here,' Carolyn says, patting the tummy flesh she's had since puberty. 'It's not that I don't have a six-pack, it's just that I've got an esky as well,' she laughs.

Jaspa strides out of the ensuite in pink and yellow floral hipster bikinis with a frilled waist and a halter-neck top, looking as photogenic as Aqua Adore's top surfer/bikini model Sky Cassidy.

'These are cute, but I'm not sure if my bum looks too floppy.' Jaspa jiggles her bottom in her hands.

'Oh, as if,' Carolyn protests, playfully throwing a

Havaiana at Jaspa, then turning towards the door as Mel comes in.

'Your butt's as floppy as a coconut,' Mel joins in, grabbing the thrown thong and using it to spank Jaspa's behind.

Carolyn slips into her khaki capris and fumbles in her bag for her zinc. 'C'mon, it's two forty-five, we've gotta bounce.'

Mel bites back a teasing 'Yo, CF from the block'. Carolyn's been dropping a lot of ghetto speak lately, probably thanks to her current obsession with '90s hip-hop.

As Jaspa, Mel and Carolyn turn the corner of main street, all looking down at their phones, they are almost bowled over by three girls from the competition circuit in full sprint. Mel pulls Jaspa and Carolyn off the pavement to avoid the stampede with only a second to spare. 'See,' Mel says, shaking her head. 'I always say phone distraction is what's going to wipe out the entire human race.'

They see Josephine Brown who is seated at a beach-front picnic table wearing a black cotton maxi dress and a pair of gold-rimmed aviator sunglasses, her hair tousled into a high bun. She looks up from her notepad and raises a hand to acknowledge the girls' arrival. Jaspa recognises the journalist from her headshot in the contributor's column of the paper – she's always thought she looks like Emma Watson. Josephine is known for a controversial story she wrote earlier in the year revealing the appalling ways some of the players from the Pacific Grove Growlers NRL team had treated women. Josephine's headline read: *We Will Not Be Silenced*. The article earned her a Walkley award.

'Hi girls, thanks for coming, take a seat. This is Sean.' Josephine points to a young man leaning against the fence, a big waterproof camera at his feet. 'He'll be doing your photo shoot today.'

Jaspa squeezes in next to Mel and Carolyn on the bench seat opposite Josephine. The contest commentary can be heard in the distance, but it's still quiet enough to talk.

Josephine places her phone on the table and taps on the My Memo app. 'We'll mainly be featuring the letter you wrote, but I'd also like to ask you a few questions, too.'

'Sure, no worries,' replies Mel.

Jaspa gives Carolyn a comforting leg squeeze under the table.

'What prompted you to write the letter?' Josephine asks, pressing record.

'We just got tired of the lack of inspiration for us as surfer girls,' Mel replies, with the confidence of someone you might see on *Oprah*. 'I mean, there's only one Australian girls' surfing publication, *Shredder*, which is more of a pamphlet attached to the back of the guys' *Line Up* magazine, and that's only produced twice a year.' Mel glances at the two girls, encouraging them to pipe in at any time.

'Yeah.' Carolyn scratches her fingernail along a groove in the wooden table. 'It's BS that even places like England have a monthly chick surf mag even though there are so many more girl rippers in Australia.'

'So, you believe it's the responsibility of the men's surfing magazines to represent female athletes?' Josephine asks, directing the question at Jaspa.

'Umm …' Jaspa leans on her hand and squints towards the sky. 'Well … I just think women's surfing is another form of beauty, and more meaningful to admire than the way someone looks.'

Mel has her mouth open, ready to add to Jaspa's response. 'I think it's the industry's responsibility to support women's surfing, and allow the public access to it. There are four men's surfing magazines in Australia and, as we say, only one "pamphlet" twice a year for women,' Mel explains, gesturing quotation marks with her fingers. 'We believe female surfing is of interest to the entire surfing community, including guys.'

Each time Jaspa considers the way females are portrayed to be ogled rather than to inspire, it's like a match lights a fire in her stomach. 'The girls on tour are incredible athletes with stories to tell. If society only showcases women as sex objects, that's not setting a good example for boys *or* girls,' Jaspa says.

Josephine checks her phone to ensure the recording

light is still on, then responds, 'That's interesting. So why isn't there a more regular magazine for surfing women?'

Carolyn remembers the manager at work telling her about *Shredder*'s beginnings. 'Oh, there was, about five years ago. *Shredder* was out every two months, like a proper mag, but it got scrapped and whacked as the add-on to *Line Up*. I hear it's cos the industry wouldn't support it with ads.'

'Oh, that's right, I used to love it!' Jaspa squeals.

Mel has her own opinion on why it didn't last. 'Did you know it was run by a bunch of guys? In fact, the pamphlet still is. Can you imagine a team of *women* running a *men's* surfing magazine?' she questions rhetorically. 'There's no way they'd allow that!' Mel unties her white cotton shirt from around her waist and slips it on, leaving it unbuttoned at the front. 'I mean, don't you reckon a women's surfing magazine would be best run by female surfers, or at least *some* female surfers?'

Jaspa crinkles her brow and nods slowly. 'Yeah, actually I do. Being a girl surfer, it's … it's different.'

'How so?' asks Josephine, who's never set foot on a board herself.

'We have boobs and butts to fit into the barrel,' Carolyn blurts, prompting a giggle and a nod of agreement from her friends.

'Well,' Jaspa says, nudging Mel with her elbow. 'It's

like what you pointed out the other morning, with the hipster.'

'Oh yeah, that's exactly it, Jazz.' Mel slams her hands on the table, almost knocking over Josephine's phone. 'Oops, sorry! So, we were out surfing yesterday and this guy paddles straight to Jaspa's inside. It's like, hello asshole, you can't act all nicey pie, say "hi" and then snake for the wave!'

Jaspa leans in to Josephine. 'To be honest, I didn't think to stand up for myself, but Mel's a good teacher,' she admits. 'I usually let guys get whatever wave they want. It can be pretty fierce out there.'

'Fully,' Carolyn adds. 'Sometimes you can smell the testosterone, it's so intense.'

Josephine sucks in air to make her cheekbones rise even higher. 'That's a great point. Do you think female surfers will always be distinctly different to males?'

Mel pops open the cap of her water bottle, takes a long gulp then offers it to Jaspa before answering. 'Well, I guess our bodies are different; we have to deal with hectic hormones. I might be ripping one day, then have my period the next and keep falling off.'

'You know what I hate?' Jaspa pushes herself against the table to lean back. 'The top pro female surfers are all absolutely ripping, doing airs, power turns and getting barrelled and the commentators always remark that they're surfing as good as the guys. Why always the comparison?'

Mel grins and pats Jaspa's hand. 'My feminist protégé, I'm so proud!'

Josephine turns off her recorder and waves at Sean to join them. 'Thank you, girls, that's great. I have more than enough now.'

Mel grins through clenched teeth. 'Sorry, I hope I didn't ramble too much.'

'Not at all. Sean, if you can take shots of the girls surfing now, and try to capture the one we spoke about.'

Mel, Jaspa and Carolyn sit on their surfboards in the ocean while the photographer floats a little further towards shore. They've already taken a few pictures on the beach. One cringeworthy shot of the three girls staring dreamily out to the horizon – the kind you always see in local newspapers, usually attracting some kind of cheesy caption like "sea change". The other pose was more fun, with them jumping in the air with their surfboards.

Sean uses his flippers to push closer towards the girls. 'For this next shot, try to choose a wave that peels, and ride it all together if you can.'

Mel splashes Jaspa. 'You know what that means?'

'Yippee! Party wave!'

Carolyn immediately paddles to position herself on the inside of Mel and Jaspa.

'Oi, what are you doing, cheeky snake?' Mel snickers, attempting to grab Carolyn's leg-rope.

For a regular surf session this would be a tactic to

have first dibs on the wave, but Carolyn's got other intentions in mind. 'What do you reckon? I wanna be furthest from the camera!'

A smaller set swoops in, offering a shoulder for them to jump on. 'This is the one, *chicas*!' screams Mel, waving her arms for them to swing their boards towards the shore.

All three jump to their feet in hysterics. Jaspa bends her knees to ride low, Mel stands tall and clasps her hands behind her back in a soul arch stance, and Carolyn grabs her rail on her backhand. While giggling and screeching, they ride along the wave, aiming at Sean, who holds his camera up high out of the water, takes a frame of photos then dives deep underneath the moving surfboards.

'I think we got it that time,' he shouts over the sound of the waves, resurfacing and flashing a smile.

Jaspa glides to catch the hands of her friends and they hold them high above their heads. 'The Bikini Collective will change the world!' she sings as they ride to shore and hop onto the sand with their hands still linked.

										#13

'Two more plates, honey, and if you can grab a couple of extra chairs from outside,' Ellen says, counting around the dining table.

Jaspa doesn't realise that with her mum, dad, Tyler, Carolyn, Mel, Mel's parents and her little brother Daniel, that still leaves one spare spot to fill.

Jaspa strides upstairs to find Carolyn sitting at the desk in their room, staring down at the phone cradled in her hands. She glances up as Jaspa comes in, but her attempted smile doesn't do a very good job of masking the fact that she's upset.

'Hey, miss, is everything okay?' Jaspa places her hands on her friend's shoulders and gives them a comforting squeeze.

'I just called Mum to tell her about the photo shoot and the GoPro, but she sounded fully wasted,' Carolyn sighs, sticking a finger between her teeth to tear off a cuticle.

'Oh, no, I'm so sorry,' Jaspa says, resting her chin on the top of Carolyn's head. 'You know, she's probably just going through a hard time at the moment.'

Carolyn relaxes under Jaspa's hands and closes her eyes to ward off any tears before they even think about making the journey down onto her cheeks. 'Yeah, you're right. She's stressing out because her hours have been cut, so we have no cash. And I reckon she gets lonely since she had to ditch Stinkbreath Steven.'

Jaspa lets out a sympathetic laugh, remembering Carolyn's mum's now-ex boyfriend. Without exaggeration, his breath smelt exactly like fresh dog doo. Carolyn used to hide out in her room whenever he visited, to avoid chance encounters with his exhalations, so she pretty much stayed there for the five months he was in their lives.

Jaspa wraps her arms around Carolyn's chest. 'We love ya, everything's going to be okay, I promise.'

Appearing at the door, Mel beckons the girls with an over-exaggerated swoop of her arm. 'I'd ask to join in on the hug-fest, but c'mon – there's a pizza party about to happen.'

They leap to their feet to follow Mel, when Jaspa hears a familiar voice downstairs say, 'Thanks for having me Mrs Ryder.'

'Oh my god, is that *Cooper*?' she whispers to Mel, freezing in her tracks.

'The one and only. And he's about to see you drip tomato sauce and cheese all down your pretty face.'

Jaspa tries to keep her cool as she approaches the remaining spare chair at the table, which is tightly nestled between Carolyn and Cooper. She kisses Mr and Mrs Appleby on the cheek on the way around, and blows a raspberry on Daniel's. 'Gross!' He winces and pulls away.

There's only a small gap between the seats, so as Jaspa slides into hers she brushes the side of Cooper's head with her chest. She's thinking: *mortification, please kill me!* He's thinking: *bonus!* Jaspa glances at Mel, who's seated directly opposite – perfectly positioned to observe highly entertaining awkward moments like this.

'Hey, Jaspa,' Cooper greets, politely pretending not to notice her embarrassment.

'Oh, hi Cooper, I didn't see it was you sitting there,' she lies terribly, folding the napkin in her lap and searching for something else to do to make her look busy.

She gestures for the water jug and he decides to pour it for her. Jaspa avoids eye contact with Mel, knowing she'll be smirking her face off right now.

'So, do you know you girls caused a bit of chaos at the coffee shop today?' Cooper asks quietly, hoping Tyler won't hear.

Mel screws up her nose, perplexed. 'Whaddaya mean? We weren't at the cafe today.'

Cooper rests on his elbow, shielding the side of his mouth with his hand and leaning closer into the triangle of girls, which is more than fine with Jaspa. *Here's my personal space, invade away.*

'You know that tool Andrew Olsen and his cronies?' The girls nod. 'They heard about the post you wrote and they were hassling Tyler about it,' he flicks his head subtly in Tyler's direction.

Jaspa lets out a soft groan, hoping this isn't something else she'll cop grief from her brother about.

Cooper holds up a hand to suggest there's more to come. 'Don't worry, he stuck up for you. But then, there was a group of chicks, the one from Sydney with the fringe …'

Mel clicks her fingers. 'Oh, yeah, umm … Pepita Map-something … Mapstone! We saw her and her friends legging it up the road today.'

'What happened?' Jaspa asks, her face now the closest to Cooper it's ever been. His breath most certainly does not smell like doggy doo.

'That Pepita girl went ballistic at the Maroubra boys, telling them to be more respectful, that girls' surfing deserves to be in the mags, and then you'll never guess what she did …' he trails off, leaving the three girls hanging.

'What? What did she do?' Carolyn demands playfully through gritted teeth, trying to keep her voice down.

'Get this, she chucked a jug of water on him in front of everyone, saying something about doing a cutback in his face. Something like that anyway. It was nuts.'

The girls gasp and giggle in disbelief. This thing has grown legs and is running rampant, way beyond what they expected.

Anthony spreads several pizza boxes along the table, and hands reach in every direction for the doughy goodness. Jaspa watches Cooper talking to her brother and father, a cute rim of oil around his lips. She remembers her first year of high school, when he was sitting with all the surfers along the surfie wall. She walked by with two of the first-grade netballers and Cooper yelled, 'Hey Jaspa, how are you, cutie?' in front of everyone. At the time it was just a friendly greeting from a guy she thought of as her older brother. She had no idea she'd one day be thinking of their mouths touching. If only she could have bottled up that moment, then open it up now and have Cooper Crawford still think she's a cutie. They could be that perfect couple who melt into each other's arms as he kisses her softly between the ear and the cheek … Mmmm …

Jaspa feels a kick to the shin under the table. Mel gestures to her to scrape a fingernail between her teeth, and Jaspa digs out a gooey clump of wilted baby spinach. 'Thanks!' she whispers, wiping it on the side of her plate not a moment too soon.

Cooper leans into her shoulder. 'What are you having?'

'Pardon?' Jaspa asks, thinking the pizza slice in her hand makes it pretty obvious she's having pizza.

'What *flavour* did you guys get?' He laughs, dropping his head in amusement.

'Oh, sorry! We got spinach, sundried tomatoes and olives. You?' She closes her lips so her tongue can slyly search for any more rogue greenery.

'Chicken and avo. Here, try some,' Cooper offers, using two hands to hold his pizza slice towards Jaspa's mouth. She parts her plump lips and takes a bite, smiling at the same time. He laughs and helps her break apart the stretchy string of cheese, then hands her his napkin. 'It's yum, yeah?'

What an understatement. This could very well be the most romantic moment of Jaspa's life. And this is only the beginning, right?

#14

Jaspa slips her arms into the pink rash vest and threads it over her head. The jagged swell looks like mini mountains on the horizon, the deep blue ocean contrasted against the pale late morning skyline. Spray from the head-high waves launching on the shore patters onto her face, leaving a salty trace around her lips.

Three girls to her left in blue, green and yellow competition shirts contort their bodies into a range of warm-up stretches. Jaspa offers them a smile, but not one returns the gesture. She hopes it's not out of meanness. Perhaps they're just not in the headspace to be exchanging greetings right now. Jaspa sits with the soles of her feet touching and her knees splayed out, tapping the sand out of her leg-rope strap.

She thinks about Carolyn, who won her third round heat by a whopping four points. Her friend seems to be cracking further out of her shell this weekend than Jaspa's ever seen. She smiles, thinking how nice it would be for Carolyn to get a lucky break in life.

Looking up from her trance, Jaspa sees that her opponents are already running towards the shore break, and hears her name being shouted behind her. Glancing back she spots Tyler, frantically pointing at the yellow flag raised above the judges' tent.

Oops, it's five minutes before the end of heat six, which means she should be paddling out into position.

'Were you waiting for a speedboat to pick you up or something?' Mel asks, as Jaspa reaches beyond the broken waves with just forty seconds to spare.

Mel secured her heat win within the first fifteen minutes, and has luck on her side – a wave lull means her competitors have no chance of catching up to her.

'I had a bit of a vague-out watching the waves. I didn't see the flag change,' Jaspa shrugs with a smile.

As the siren sounds to end her heat, Mel starts the paddle towards shore. 'Seriously, Jaspa, this is not the time to be spacing out. You've gotta get your game together!'

Jaspa attempts to unravel the knot in her stomach as Mel's criticism pulls it tighter. She looks at her borrowed watch to see that ten minutes have flown by already and her feet haven't even touched the board yet. The strong offshore wind makes it easy for Jaspa to hear the scores of yellow in first place with a 5.5, blue in second with 5.3, green in third on four points, and pink on zero.

She notices her chance to get out of fourth place almost too late as a right-hander rises up beneath her, jolting her out of her thoughts. The girl down the line to her right in blue begins to paddle, thinking there's no way Jaspa can make the drop. With no time to be picky, Jaspa takes two short strokes into the wave, springs to her feet, freefalling with the pitching lip and offers a polite, 'Yep, got it!' to prevent a drop-in from her opponent.

She reaches the bottom of the wave with a thud, but her low stance stops her from sliding out. Instead, the speed of her take-off allows for a dynamic bottom turn. She soars into the top pocket of the wave, but it's breaking down on her too fast to be able to pull off a re-entry. Before Jaspa even realises her movements, she snaps the board underneath her to position herself tightly under the curling lip. A crowd-pleasing barrel opens around her and for five seconds all onlookers can see is a whoosh of pink behind the blue curtain. For a moment, Jaspa feels time stand still as a blanket of ocean shields her, and the outside world is silenced. She savours every microsecond in the belly of the wave before reaching the light and gliding out to finish off her ride with two critical turns.

Jaspa paddles down the beach, away from the main peak where her competitors scrap for waves. The corners of her mouth curl and she playfully slaps the water on hearing the score of her only ride echo out across the ocean. Even someone not savvy with tallies knows that a 9.5 is a near-perfect start.

As Jaspa strokes through the water towards her second wave, she realises she's no longer alone. A flash of yellow darts to her inside and before Jaspa has a chance to launch to her feet, Tara Watson yells that it's *her* wave. Jaspa jerks back her board and raises her eyebrows in disbelief as Tara slices her fins into the lip so hard that a cover of spray blasts into Jaspa's face.

For the remainder of the heat, she can't escape Tara. Whenever Jaspa paddles for a potentially heat-winning wave, Tara cuts her off and claims it for herself. Jaspa sighs. *Is she doing this on purpose?* Just as Jaspa is convinced she's allowed herself to be bullied out of the competition and out of the race for the junior tour qualification, she's stunned to hear that she's finished in second place. If she can progress through a heat by catching just one wave, imagine what she could do with two.

Tara is chitchatting away to Jaspa as they walk towards the officials' area to return their rashies. Jaspa lets Tara babble on about how the swell's getting bigger and it's going to be sick, and how it's just like her local spot at home and that Jaspa should come down and visit her in Newy one day … Only five minutes ago Tara was practically sitting on top of Jaspa's board to make sure she couldn't catch a wave, and now she's nicey-pie. What's with that?

Jaspa spies Cooper in the distance pulsing up and down on his toes and whirling his arms like propellers. She guesses he must be preparing for his heat and wonders if he gets intimidated, too. Cutting off Tara mid-sentence, Jaspa says a timid goodbye and heads in Cooper's direction. She feels much more relaxed about him after last night. Surely he'll try to kiss her in the near future? No one feeds you pizza like *that* if they think of you like a little sister.

In their room after dinner, Carolyn convinced Jaspa that he's definitely keen, and suggested she should show him that she is, too, before some other girl does. A tingle dances up the back of Jaspa's neck as she remembers the sly wink Cooper gave her when he was talking to her dad at the other end of the table, and how his warm lips melted into her cheek like marshmallow as he said goodbye.

As the clouds part, rays from the early morning sun prickle across Jaspa's skin, her eyelids relaxed and heavy from its heat. She combs her fingers through her wet locks to smooth them out and a subtle swing creeps into her hips. Her heart palpitates as she gets nearer, like the moment you see a wave coming towards you that's a little bigger than you're comfortable with, knowing you just have to go for it because it's too perfect to let go.

'Hi Cooper,' she waves, eager to wish him luck,

hoping she'll be brave enough to make plans to catch up later. Perhaps they could even go surfing together, she thinks, completely forgetting she's got a quarter final to compete in.

Jaspa notices Cooper's shoulders stiffen. He doesn't even wait for her to reach his side before offering an abrupt, 'I can't talk right now,' and taking off towards the ocean.

A wave of embarrassment and disappointment washes over Jaspa as she's left standing alone on the sand in disbelief. One tear trickles down her face, glides to the corner of her mouth and dives off her chin, prompting more to follow. Jaspa throws her rash vest into the returns bin without making eye contact with anyone. If ambushed, at least she can blame her blood-shot eyes on the salt water. Everyone at her tent is probably wondering where she is, but she can't face a soul right now. Mel's mad at her, Cooper brushed her off, she's getting hassled in heats … she rests her board on the ground and slumps on the grass against a gum tree with a sigh. Placing her face in her hands, she allows the tears to stream down her cheeks.

#15

Something warm and wet splats onto the back of Jaspa's hand. She unburies her face from between her folded arms and sees a mass of white goo trickling down her fingers and onto her wrist as a kookaburra cackles on the branch above.

'Oh dear, he got you a beauty,' she hears someone croak from behind. She turns to see a lady who must be about sixty, seated on a park bench Jaspa hadn't noticed. The lady digs into her handbag and offers her a bunch of tissues. Jaspa's not sure if they're meant for the bird poop or her tears, but she reaches over to accept them.

'Thank you,' she says, using them to first wipe her face, then hand. 'I … I … didn't notice you were there,' she mumbles, not sure how much of her sniffling and blubbering the lady has overheard.

'I don't mean to pry, but is everything all right?' the lady asks in a low voice.

'Yeah …' Jaspa replies unconvincingly, sucking in her cheeks in an attempt to force the emotion back down.

'You know, sometimes talking to someone you have no connection to can be a big help. The amount of baggage I've unleashed on strangers would fill an aircraft,' the lady laughs. She pats the space on the bench next to her.

Jaspa takes a seat and offers her hand. 'I'm Jaspa, lovely to meet you.'

'Likewise, Jaspa. I'm Rosie. Rosie Kay.' She points towards the surfboard on the grass. 'Is that yours? Are you in the competition?'

Jaspa stares down at her board, the inanimate object that's caused her equal measures of pleasure and pain over the past month. 'Yeah, it's mine. I'm competing, but I … well … sometimes I feel like I just don't belong here, you know?'

'Well, yes. I've been watching some of it, as my granddaughter is in the event. She's only thirteen, it's her first year. There are a lot of talented surfers this season, is that what's bothering you?'

'No. I mean, yes, kind of.' Jaspa props her knees up against her chest and wraps her arms around them. 'It's not that I don't think I can surf as well as them. I mean,

I used to think I couldn't, but it seems I can … it's just, I'm wired differently to the other competitors. They seem to have an agenda; training, strategies … all I want to do is surf. I'm just not sure I'm cut out for all of the rules.'

'Jaspa, I can relate to your feelings more than you know.' Rosie is smiling, and nods before drawing in a deep breath. 'I was a surfer in the seventies. I could've had it all. I was winning almost every event I entered, and starting to attract interest from sponsors wanting to take me on the professional tour. But before it even began, I walked away.'

Jaspa is mesmerised. She doesn't want to seem pushy, but she needs to know more. 'What happened? Where did you go?'

Rosie clasps her hands, folding her fingers over the wrinkles in her knuckles, and rests them in her lap. 'I climbed up onto my high horse and galloped off to Byron Bay to be a hippie. I didn't think it was possible to be a competitive surfer *and* a soul surfer all in one.'

Jaspa's mouth drops open in disbelief. 'That's exactly what's in my head right now!' she squeals, smacking her forehead with the heel of her hand.

'Well, let me tell you, while I don't regret moving to Byron and meeting my husband and having a beautiful daughter, I now believe you can do both. You can put your soul and your own flavour into all aspects of surfing.' The lines around Rosie's eyes fold into kind creases and she rests a hand on Jaspa's knee. 'That's something I tell my granddaughter. Every surfer is an individual, there is no right or wrong. Just stay true to yourself and all will be perfect.'

'Do you have any regrets?'

'I've never been out of Australia. I gave up the chance to travel the world and experience all it has to offer. That's definitely something I wish I hadn't walked away from.'

'So you're saying I could be on the world tour, but do it my way?'

'If that's what makes you feel good, then it sounds like a pretty great plan to me.'

Jaspa flops back against the bench and smiles. 'I have always wanted to go to Hawaii, and Malibu and Brazil,' she ponders. 'Especially if that means going with my best friends. I can't believe I let myself get so upset about this,' she says, swinging her legs to propel herself forward. 'I'm such an emo!'

'I'm not sure what that is, but you are what you are, and that's all you need to remember.'

Jaspa bends down to give Rosie a hug, then picks up her surfboard and strides towards the tent.

Carolyn is leaning on the beach side of the fence. 'Hey, yo, where've you been?'

'Oh, there was a massive line for the loo, took ages,' Jaspa lies.

Carolyn takes Jaspa's surfboard so she can climb over the fence. 'Tyler's about to surf his quarter final, and yours isn't long after that. Dude, everyone thought you were gonna miss it.'

She smiles, jumping from the rail onto the sand. 'Nah, I'm just on Jaspa time.'

#16

Tyler paddles furiously into his first wave of the heat. His three opponents watch as he takes off on a hollow left-hander, squats low, cuts into a speedy bottom turn and then sprays a massive backside manoeuvre. Not shifting from his low stance, Tyler performs two more risk-taking turns and ends the wave with a deep six-second sand barrel. As he's shot forward from beneath the cover of water, he screams, 'Yeah!' and pumps his fist towards the judges.

Opinion blares from the speakers declaring Tyler's the stronger surfer of this heat, and a likely shoo-in to go the whole way in this competition. The judges agree, rewarding him with a 9.8 and the crowd goes nuts, with his family screeching and whistling from the sand.

As he's paddling back out, Tyler sees the surfer in blue get an impressive ride, achieving a combination of three solid turns and popping an aerial to complete the wave. When Tyler hears his opponent's score of 8.5, he clenches his teeth tight enough to shatter them. There's no way he's allowing this kook to beat him.

All Tyler needs is a second placing in this heat and he'll secure enough points to qualify for the junior tour. But he's hungry for a win, the glory of a win. The announcement that Cooper had progressed to the semi finals plays over in Tyler's mind, leaving him breathless and more psyched than ever. The plan, ever since joining the Bonita Shores Boardriders when the boys could barely stand on a surfboard, is to both qualify for the World Junior Tour. Neither has considered the possibility that only one of them might make it.

Tyler stays within half a metre of the challenger in blue at all times. They hassle each other into rides, which only attract scores in the low range. The other two competitors go wave-for-wave on the smaller right-hand break, their average six-point scores not even on Tyler's radar. A set approaches, and Tyler paddles to the far right of his rival to get himself into position. With a smirk on his face and a boost of adrenaline, he strokes into the five footer, rising with the thick wall of water ready to set himself up for the biggest wave of the day so far, sure to be a heat winner. Grabbing the outside rail of his surfboard, Tyler soars down the water feeling like he's speed-bombing a hill on his skatey. For a few seconds he has a clear view of the direction he wants to take, an overhead blanket of blue outstretched like an empty highway. He stamps on his front foot to gain speed then gasps as a thick section of the wave suddenly shuts down, the lip smacking him into the shallow sand bank and holding him there for several seconds. The surfer in blue is far enough down the line to take off in perfect position, and puts on a dynamic display of power surfing that sees him rewarded with eight points from the judges.

Tyler pushes himself off the sand and swims furiously to the surface. He fills his lungs just before the set of waves strikes him back down. Pulling on his leg-rope, he draws his board towards him, hops on and paddles strongly towards the back of the line-up.

The scores are announced, and although Tyler has clocked up the highest single wave of the heat, his best two-wave combination has him only in third place. Panic floods him as his watch blinks – there are only four minutes remaining in the heat. Tyler swears and aggressively kicks his legs to power-paddle back into position. Straddling his surfboard, all he can do is wait for his elusive last ride. He punches the water in frustration as the surfers placed first and second turn Tyler's tactics against him, sitting less than a metre away, ready to challenge his every movement.

Back on the beach, the commentary team feed off the drama and wind up the crowd like a yo-yo. Surf journalists take particular interest in the heat, knowing that an upset like this is sure to attract a punchy head-line and plenty of online shares.

Jaspa and her family scream encouragement from their tent, fearing that Tyler's about to hit the post of his lifelong goal.

'C'mon Huey, give us a set!' Anthony bellows through cupped hands, calling on the surfing god.

'Tyler Ryder is in third place. He needs a 3.5 to get into second, or a 7.5 to move into first,' the commentator blares over the loudspeaker.

Jaspa hugs her mum around the shoulders and buries her head against her neck. 'He should just take off on anything, he can get that score with his eyes shut!' she says.

Tyler feels a tightness in his chest, a sense of urgency. He allows one of his opponents to hassle him out of two waves that roll through, knowing they'll shut down again, leaving him without enough time to return to the back of the line-up.

A small right-hander makes its way towards the shallows. Looking at his watch, Tyler realises he needs to take this ride, no matter what. Only forty seconds remain in the heat. All he needs to qualify for the launch pad of his surfing career is a 3.5 – just two of his most average turns. That should be a cinch, and he's absolutely pumped to end this heat with the most magnificent and nail-biting climax of the competition so far.

Tyler knows he's the better surfer, with the ability to take off deeper than the others, so he scoots himself into position and jumps to his feet with the confidence of someone who plans to tear the wave apart. Racing to avoid the shut-down section, Tyler leans hard into a stylish turn at the bottom of the wave that generates so much speed, the ensuing dynamic top turn he sets himself up for will be enough on its own for the required score. He shifts weight to his front foot to swivel the board around, but as he returns the pressure to his back foot to slice his fins through the breaking water, he slips on the wax and collapses onto his board with a thud. His body is flung over the falling lip and he's tumbled underwater like a ragdoll, his pro-surfing hopes breaking with the wave itself.

#17

'Should we go and talk to him?' Jaspa asks her mum, having just witnessed Tyler's meltdown on the beach in front of the judges' area – and the world, it seems, given the amount of phones that were held up to capture the moment. Jaspa wonders how two humans can be created by the same people but turn out so differently. Perhaps he got her share of the hothead gene?

'No, let's leave him be. And don't take it to heart if he doesn't want to talk about it,' Ellen says, dusting sand off her water bottle and taking a delicate sip before changing the subject. 'How's Mel doing? This is her quarter final, yes?'

Jaspa takes off her oversized sunglasses and squints towards the ocean at the girls' competition area. 'Yep. She's doing okay, I'm pretty sure. Carolyn?' she asks her friend, who's folded forward in a stretch.

'Yeah, looks like she'll romp it in. There's only a minute to go,' Carolyn replies while gripping her ankles.

The siren sounds and Jaspa claps, happy for Mel's win and relieved, too – that's one less of the known fire-starters in her life whose emotions could blaze out of control because of a surfing contest. 'Let's go down and congratulate her,' Jaspa suggests. 'We'll be back soon, Mum, my quarter final is in about an hour.' She takes Carolyn by the hand and runs to the shore.

'Ready?' Jaspa asks, submerging her arms in the water. Carolyn nods and they wait until Mel is a few feet away before pelting her with sand drops.

'Right biatches, you're goin' down!' Mel screams, ditching her surfboard and freeing her hands for retaliation.

They dive under the breaking waves together to wash off and Carolyn places her hands on her knees to catch her breath. 'Nice surfing, Mel, you dominated that heat. I've gotta shoot, I'm in the third quarters. Any tips?'

'Yeah, don't always go for the sets – some of 'em are closing out,' Mel advises, tucking her board back under her arm.

Jaspa and Mel wish Carolyn luck as she jogs up the beach to collect her competition vest. 'That's what Tyler just struggled with, the closeouts,' Jaspa says as she walks with Mel to the officials' area. She's dumb-founded that people like Tyler and Mel can even try to predict something like winning a competition when it hinges on something as unpredictable as a breaking wave.

'Wait, you mean he didn't make it?' Mel stops, grabbing Jaspa's arm. 'I thought he was a dead cert for his heat.'

Jaspa hangs her head, feeling the weight of her brother's disappointment and struggling to work out how she can console him without sounding condescending. 'He was ripping, absolutely ripping, but he started hassling and seemed to lose it a bit out there.' The girls walk slowly up the beach, a fog of sorrow following them. 'He would've just scraped through but he fell on his last ride. He only needed a 3.5.'

'Man, that's so heavy. So he can't qualify now?'

Jaspa shakes her head. 'Nope, I think it's over. He'll have to do all the local comps and try again next year.'

'Seriously, Jaspa, I feel way bad for Tyler, but you should stay the hell outta his way for the rest of the day. You don't want him ruining your surfing story.'

Jaspa nods sadly. She knows she's the last thing Tyler needs right now – and vice versa.

* * *

Jaspa stares at the closed bathroom door. As soon as her quarter final had finished, she bolted straight back to the house to be alone, her guilt following closely behind.

Jaspa cradles two bits of paper in the palm of her hand. She stares at them blankly.

Talk to him, he needs you.

Leave him be, he'll come to you when he's ready.

Heaviness weighs in her chest, that feeling of not being able to help someone, especially when they're forever pushing you away. Her brother has had his hopes crushed, and she's scared to utter two words to him. She wants to wrap her arms around him and reassure him that everything will be okay, that this must've happened for a reason. Humph, that'd go down as well as a broken elevator.

Tyler has had his sights firmly fixed on being a pro surfer since his first contest win, when he was just nine years old. And he has the potential to do it, but the feedback along the way has always been the same: he'll have to work hard at it. He will never be one of those people who finds it easy, someone with a natural grace, whose every move pops into sync perfectly, who possesses a deep, soulful connection with the ocean. Unlike someone else in his family who just won her quarters.

Jaspa is startled by a repetitive banging, which sounds like a round of bullets.

'What are you doing in there, having a nervous poo?' Mel shouts through the toilet door. 'Why didn't you wait for me?'

'I'll be done in a minute,' Jaspa replies, fully clothed and sitting on top of the closed seat.

'We've gotta go – like, seriously, the semis are starting soon. I'll see you out the front.' Mel retreats back downstairs and sits on the front bench, jiggling her leg impatiently.

Jaspa screws up the paper in her hand, shuts her eyes and unfolds one of the strips. Her gut instinct is right, and the universe agrees – now is not the time. She's just going to have to accept that Tyler doesn't need her right now.

'Sorry, I didn't mean to take so long. Here,' Jaspa offers, chucking Mel a banana.

'Thanks. Don't eat it now, though. Last thing we need is nana vommies in the semi finals,' Mel says as they walk across the street towards their beach tent.

'How did Carolyn go?' Jaspa asks, tucking the banana into her bag.

'She made the semis, which means she's qualified already! Mad, huh?' Mel nudges Jaspa with her elbow. 'So, how you feeling? Are you pumped? This is huge, Jazz, we've almost made it, too.'

Before Jaspa can come up with a convincing answer, an argument stops them in their tracks. A girl storms towards the beach, trying to escape her dad's outrage. Jaspa recognises her as Lisa Campbell, one of the competitors in her quarter final, who only just scraped into second place. Although her placing means she has still made it through to the semi finals, it obviously wasn't enough to impress her father.

'You let her out-surf you, and you were bogging most of your turns,' her dad thunders, saliva flying. 'All the money I've spent on coaching you goes out the window when you don't listen,' he shouts, tugging at his earlobe to illustrate his point.

'Look!' Lisa screams, raising the palm of her hand to her forehead in frustration. 'I made it through, I don't know why you're stressing over this. This is *my* dream, not yours. Just because you're a has-been. Get off my back!' Lisa bolts.

Having a dad who's an ex-junior state champion should be a blessing for any surfer, but not for Lisa. When her dad was Lisa's age he was their hometown's surfing hero, Jan Juc's biggest hope of making a splash on the world surfing stage. But that was during an era when many professional surfers indulged in hard partying while competing, and only a handful could juggle that combination successfully. Despite years of trying, and using every dollar he had, Lisa's dad never made it past the top sixty surfers in the world. He concluded his attempt with no cash, little education and wound up with a job he loathes, looking ten years older than he is. His little girl is his only chance of surfing stardom.

'Man, I bicker with my mum, but you gotta feel

grateful not to have to put up with that crap,' Mel whispers to Jaspa.

'I know, poor thing,' Jaspa agrees, wiping her sunglasses on her dress. 'Must be so embarrassing for her. She seems pretty nice, too. Remember we met her at that event on Phillip Island in March?'

'Yeah, that was one of the funnest comps this year, I reckon,' Mel nods. 'I do recall her dad having a bit of a spat there as well. Didn't he storm into the judges' area?'

'Yep. I hear the association even threatened to ban him from events. I bet she wants to qualify just to get away from him.'

'Female surfers in the semi finals, please check in. Action starts in fifteen minutes,' a voice bellows over the loudspeaker.

Mel squeals in excitement and pulls Jaspa towards the tents, where they each collect a rash vest. Mel is in blue and will be in semi final one. Jaspa will be wearing yellow in the second semi with Carolyn. Jaspa takes a sly peek at the men's heat sheets to see that Cooper has just qualified for the final. If she was his girlfriend they could support one another. She could even stand on the sand and point out where the sets are coming from and direct him to the best waves. When they get married and buy a beach house, they can have one side of the mantel for his trophies and the other for hers, with a photo of them riding tandem on a longboard at sunrise hanging above it. Jaspa snaps out of her daydream with a twist in her stomach as she realises that this picture is most unlikely to come to life.

A hand lands on her shoulder and she draws in a sharp breath and lets out a little squeak.

'Oops, sorry Jaspa, I didn't realise you were miles away!' the man laughs. 'Hope you pay more attention in your semi,' he jokes. Jaspa is thrilled to see it's Thomas Sampson, the head surf coach at her school, the Institute of Sporting Excellence.

'Mr Sampson, you scared the bejeezus out of me!' Jaspa giggles, steadying her breath. She's grateful to have bumped into her teacher. He, more than anyone, gets where she's coming from with her surfing. She makes a mental note to tell him about her earlier encounter with Rosie, and how it helped put being a competitive surfer into perspective.

'I've been watching your heats, girls. I'm really proud, and whatever happens from here, you should be really proud, too.' Thomas has a particular interest in Jaspa's journey. She's not the most tactical on his team, but she's definitely the most naturally gifted, and has a unique relationship with the ocean.

'What's going to happen from here is that we're going to make it through and join Carolyn on the tour, that's what's happening,' Mel states matter-of-factly.

'Well, you've definitely got all the tools you need to achieve that, Mel. You're both surfing incredibly. Just remember how to use positioning to your advantage and to really read the waves. Conditions are getting trickier with the tide change and the increasing swell,' he says, nodding towards the ocean.

'I know, I've been grilling Jaspa about not getting hassled out of position,' Mel says with the best of intentions, albeit bossy ones.

Jaspa grins and nods, there's no point arguing. She has her own strategy of listening to the ocean, and surfing as though she's the only one in the line-up, but trying to explain that would be futile – she'd just get laughed at.

'Well, you girls best go and prepare. I'll be down on the beach before you paddle out. They've held off the boys' finals until after the girls have surfed, so I'm all yours,' Thomas says with a sweep of his arms. 'Jaspa, ask Tyler to give me a call so we can offer him some counselling services. I'm sure he's devastated,' he adds softly.

'Thanks, I'll definitely let Mum and Dad know,' Jaspa replies. There's no way in hell she's going to tell Tyler to get counselling. She sighs to herself, hoping her big brother isn't losing it too much.

$$\#18$$

'She didn't commit enough to her first turn, there's no way she'll get more than a 6.5,' says the girl in green.

'It'll be close, but she's totally out-surfed them the entire heat. It's only fair she gets through,' the surfer in pink says.

As the siren sounds to begin their semi finals battle, Jaspa listens to her competitors speculate on the fate of Mel's final wave from the previous heat. Having found herself in third place with only fifty-four seconds remaining and needing a 7.2 to move into second, Mel scrambled into a set wave. As the five-minute flag was raised and Jaspa paddled out for her semi final, she saw Mel take off with a bit of wobble before finding her groove to complete a four-turn combination of an off-the-top re-entry, round house cutback into the pocket, then another off-the-top before finishing with an ally-oop aerial. But what if it wasn't enough? Would Mel be genuinely happy for Jaspa and Carolyn if they made the tour without her? Jaspa would like to think so.

'Yo, focus, focus,' Carolyn says, snapping her fingers at Jaspa. 'Quit worrying, we'll find out soon enough.'

Jaspa diverts her eyes away from the shore, where she can just make out Mel pacing in front of the judges' area like a panther. 'Right, I guess we should think about catching our own waves!' she says, smiling at Carolyn. 'I'm just crossing everything Mel gets through so she has the chance to qualify with you.'

A surge of water swells up onto the sandbank, making a beeline for Jaspa. For a moment she thinks the wave has crept up on her too quickly and considers pulling back, then thinks, *all that will do is fill me with regret. What if, what IF I just went for it?* As the lip of the wave throws itself towards the beach, Jaspa presses her hands into the board to stand tall, her feet freefalling, not connecting to the waxed deck until she lands with a thump at the bottom of the wave. With her back to the foam, Jaspa jams her right foot so her fins slice through the ocean like razors, then collapses her back knee and grabs the board's outside rail to race through the tunnel. A sheet of ocean whirls around her – it's one of the best barrel rides of her surfing existence. The wave spits her out like a stone from a slingshot and Jaspa's tummy churns as she's propelled forward, finishing the ride with a series of four snaps that sees the nose of her board seamlessly reach beyond twelve o'clock. As Jaspa hears the commentators cut short their enthusiasm over her ride to announce the results of Mel's heat, she sits on her board and stares towards the beach without a blink.

'Thanks for your patience, folks. We now have the final scores for the women's first semi final.' The crowd falls silent. Jaspa closes her eyes and holds her breath.

'Melissa, your final wave scored a 7.5!'

The crowd goes nuts as the announcer continues. 'Final results are: Lisa Campbell in first place, Melissa Appleby in second place – you'll both be moving through to the final,' the commentator continues. 'Commiserations to Rebecca Oldfield in third and Tara Watson in fourth. However, Tara still qualifies for next year's tour. Congratulations!'

Jaspa grins and swings her board around just in time for Carolyn to soar over her on a cloud of foam.

'Yew, did ya hear that?' Carolyn screeches as her head pops up from the water like a bobbed apple. 'Mel freakin' made the final!'

Jaspa stops paddling and turns to face Carolyn, one eye on the lookout for sets. 'I know, I'm so excited for her! Hey, I'll see you out the back,' she says, drawing her palm through the ocean and pushing it underneath her board to steer herself forward.

'Actually, you won't,' Carolyn smirks. 'I've got a little problem to contend with, so you get out there and nail this semi!' Carolyn waves a broken board over her head, hyping up the crowd, who respond with a cheer. A soft giggle escapes Jaspa and she smiles to herself, thinking how lucky she is to call these incredible girls her friends.

At the end of her heat, Jaspa doesn't bother to return her rashie, instead running straight towards Mel and Carolyn, who are sitting on the fence behind her parents' tent. Over the sound of sand squeaking between her toes, Jaspa can hear their hoots and cheers getting louder.

'You slayed that heat, you style-master!' Mel beams, springing from the rail to embrace Jaspa. 'Check this out for BuzzFeed-worthy commentary,' she adds, handing her phone to Jaspa, who looks down at Mel's status update:

The top seven reasons semi two rocked!
The waves are cranking. Nuff said.
This is hands-down the best girls' surfing I've seen this year.
My homie **Carolyn Fitzgerald** charged a huge foam-ball floater.
Sure, the floater broke **Carolyn Fitzgerald**'s board, but this little legend has qualified for the tour. Yew!
I saw a flash of lightning far out to sea and it was spectacular.

*My bestie **Jaspa Ryder** just surfed as stylishly as ever to come second …*

… this means she's in the finals with meeeeeeee!

A bubble of happiness bursts from Jaspa's heart to leap up into her throat and a tear rolls down her cheek, collecting ocean drops along the way. 'You ripped too, Mel. I saw your last wave and held my breath until I heard your score. I almost passed out!' Jaspa picks up Carolyn's surfboard to inspect the nose, which flaps precariously on a thin film of fibreglass. 'Whoa, you got your money's worth out of that snap! I'm sorry you didn't make it through, though.'

Carolyn leans on her hands and draws her feet underneath her to balance on the rail. 'Yeah, but I'm stoked because now I can relax and cheer for both of you in the final. I am bummed about the board, but my boss said I could replace it for free.'

'What a legend, that's so generous of her. Plus, you know there are plenty of spares in our shed, take your pick!' Jaspa says, wrapping Mel's towel around her shoulders.

'Jazz, let's go, we've gotta check in for the final. Watch this for me please, *amiga*,' Mel says, chucking her backpack to land underneath Carolyn.

Jaspa holds up a hand. 'I'll catch you in two secs, I just wanna say hi to Mum and Dad.' Bounding towards the tent, she stops short when she sees Tyler approaching. Her dad gives him a back-slapping hug.

'You should be very proud. You surfed fantastically, and that's all you can do,' Anthony says while Ellen offers Tyler a veggie patty sandwich.

Tyler grumbles a sort-of acknowledgement and takes a massive bite. 'What's going on with the girls?' he asks through a mouthful of bread in a mumble only a mother could decipher.

'Mel just scraped through into the final, and Carolyn and Jaspa just finished their semi,' Ellen replies.

Tyler swallows down his jealousy. 'What do they need to get to make it through, then?' he grunts.

'Carolyn has already qualified by making it to the semis. Mel needs a third in the final,' Ellen says.

'And Jaspa still has a lot of work ahead of her. She needs to win the event,' Anthony interjects.

Tyler snorts condescendingly. 'Looks like we're both on the bench next year, then.'

Those last words knock the wind from Jaspa. She can't believe her own flesh and blood would rather see her fail than succeed without him. Tyler's tantrums are beginning to wear thinner than her one-mil springsuit. Gritting her teeth, Jaspa heaves a silent sigh and creeps away without being noticed – something she might need to get used to, considering all the eggshells she seems to be walking over lately. Shaking her head, she jogs to the contest area, deciding it's time to quit guilt-tripping herself.

The final starts in fifteen minutes. She deserves to be there.

Bring. It. On.

#19

There's a photo on the event's Instagram showing Mel, Jaspa, Pepita and Lisa all in their competition vests holding their surfboards under their arms. The caption reads: *Wiloonga Junior finalists hit the waves in fifteen minutes. Go girls!* The photo doesn't get nearly as many comments as the one that was posted a couple of hours earlier showing Tyler chucking his board, his top teeth biting down on his bottom lip just before he'd fired off a round of f-bombs. The caption reads: *Ten bucks says Tyler Ryder is not mouthing 'fabulous' as he waves goodbye to next year's World Junior Tour.*

Jaspa and Mel walk down towards the shoreline. The sand is starting to cool as the sun makes its descent, currently hovering over the Bungaloo mountain ranges. Jaspa's grin widens. While she mightn't be too fussed about the hassling and sly tactics that can come with competing, she's definitely buzzing on her achieve-ments, way more than she ever imagined. When she surfs a wave well it isn't ego that fuels her ambition. She doesn't particularly care if anyone thinks she's good or not. It's the feeling of reading a wave perfectly, of putting yourself in risky positions but knowing the ocean well enough to trust that she'll be okay, that's what she's addicted to. Imagine being able to do all that *and* travel the world with her two best friends …

'Hey,' Mel interrupts Jaspa's daydream. 'I know it's daunting that you need to win this event, but you've got this,' she continues, picking up the slack in her leg-rope. 'Just make sure you surf a smart heat, okay?'

'Sure Mel, I promise. You, too,' Jaspa replies, before placing her hand on Mel's forearm. 'Wait up a sec.' Jaspa turns to face Pepita and Lisa, who are walking 50 metres behind them.

'Hi,' Jaspa greets them as they get within hearing distance. 'I'm Jaspa, I don't think we've formally met.'

Mel rolls her eyes and keeps walking. Jaspa's clearly not adhering to her 'no friends in a final' rule – best friends excluded, naturally.

'I'm Pepita – Pep – this is Lisa.' Pep has scrunched up the sleeves on her pink rashie like a muscle shirt and her black hair is pulled into a blunt ponytail that sprouts from the back of her neck. 'We heard about the *Salt Action* post. Nice one,' Pep offers dryly, not allowing the conversation to flow much further. Her deadpan voice sounds like it only travels from the back of her throat. The kind you hear from the indie city chicks. *Probably because she is a city chick*, thinks Jaspa, albeit more punk-indie than cardigan-wearing, craft-making indie.

If it wasn't for surfing, Pepita Mapstone could very well be one of the best drummers in Sydney. Her high school band, No Kitty Bad Kitty, were winners of triple j's Unearthed High competition two years ago, and scored a record deal with Stealth Music shortly after. But pretty soon her musical and surfing careers were running neck and neck around the track of success, neither getting ahead of the pack. She decided to take a break from the band to concentrate on surf comps in an attempt to qualify for the junior tour. Making it past the quarter final means she's done just that.

Her kickass stick skills aren't exactly wasted, though. Her main sponsor, Volcom, use shots of her drumming as part of their Wild Things campaign; a series featuring their team riders surfing on one side of the page, usually popping an air, then shredding at their out-of-water passions on the other. She's in the company of graffiti artists, motocross riders, other musos, parkour enthusiasts and more.

Realising the conversation has dwindled to dead air, Jaspa smiles and waves goodbye, which in truth feels awkward, given she's only a few inches away. It's like the moment you home in for a first kiss, then hesitate at the last minute, thinking, cheek or lips? Lips or cheek?

'Good luck,' Jaspa offers, before finding her own sand space. She stretches out her legs, flexes her feet and leans forward to fold her fingers over her toes. 'They seem lovely,' she says, craning her neck to look at Mel.

'I'm sure,' Mel replies bluntly, twisting to face away from Jaspa.

Mel shivers and shakes out her shoulders.

'Are you nervous?' Jaspa asks lightheartedly. She's about to surf with just three other people in the water, she can't wait!

'No,' Mel snaps. 'Look, just make sure you win this damn final, okay?' She stands up and pads down the velcro of her leg-rope, shooting her a look that suggests if Jaspa falls short, Mel will have no hesitation in swooping in like a seagull stealing a chip from its buddy to claim victory.

The four finalists straddle their boards. The sea rises and falls like the belly of a sleeping giant. They hold their collective breaths and are blanketed by an eerie calm as they wait for the first person to catch a wave.

Pepita breaks away fast from the pack to power-stroke into a sizey left-hander. Her competitors watch from the back of the wave as she disappears down the face, leaving a series of sprays to bookmark where she's been.

Mel and Jaspa are in position to take the second and third waves in the set. Mel slices hers to pieces with several vertical backhand attacks of risky in-the-pocket positioning. Jaspa's graceful ballerina-like turns mesmerise the crowd as she links flawlessly from re-entries and cutbacks to floaters and tube rides. Any doubts about her power ability are quashed each time water explodes from beneath her board.

Mel, Jaspa and Pepita continue a wave-for-wave exchange over the next twenty minutes, with less than two points between third and first place. And then it happens: Jaspa makes the mistake of paddling over to where Lisa is positioned.

'Oh geez, what's wrong?' Jaspa asks, seeing Lisa sobbing into her hands.

Lisa draws in a breath and explains in a quivering voice that she's yet to even catch a wave. That means once she's back on dry land, crap will hit the fan, all at the hands of her father. 'He's gonna lose it. It's bad enough that I'm going to come last, but to not even post a score … oh man,' she whimpers, shaking her head.

Jaspa grabs the nose of Lisa's board and draws the two of them closer together. 'You're in the final. You should be stoked about that, and I'm sure your dad will be, too.'

'You don't know hi—' Lisa begins, but she's cut off by an announcement.

'Lisa Campbell in blue, you are yet to score. Pepita Mapstone in pink you're in third on 15.4. Jaspa Ryder in green, you currently hold second position on 16.5, and Melissa Appleby, in yellow, you are the heat leader on 16.8. Surfer in green, in order to progress into first place you need to better an 8.3. Competitors, there are seven minutes remaining.'

Jaspa lets go of Lisa's board as she spots a perfectly-formed right-hander storming in towards her like a freight train. She's on the inside of Lisa with priority. The wave is pitching in exactly the right spot along the rip bank in a way that could see it run for 50 metres or more. Jaspa's belly is bubbling with excitement – this is her chance to try for first place. She swings her board to assume take-off position, but before she even realises what she's doing, before realising she's about to make the biggest mistake of her life, she pulls back and screams at Lisa to take the wave.

20

A rock smashes against the beachside fence, thrown by a furious Tyler. He screams expletives through gritted teeth and kicks over an empty esky, knocking it into the gazebo.

'Tyler,' Ellen warns, 'watch your mouth, there are kids around. That is *not* okay behaviour.'

'She doesn't even give a crap, Mum. She's so close to getting through … she's an ungrateful little bitch!' Tyler flinches as his dad swings around to face him.

'Right, you. One more word and we'll stick you on a bus straight back to Bonita Shores tonight. It's time you started worrying about your own life. Quit hassling Jaspa about hers.' Anthony's disciplinary button isn't pushed easily – you know you're in trouble when his voice rises above 80 decibels.

Tyler fumbles around, noisily stuffing things into his

backpack. 'Well, looks like she's a loser, too. I'm outta here.' He kicks his feet into his thongs and storms off.

Anthony squeezes Ellen around the shoulder and kisses her temple. 'It's not over yet,' he mumbles to himself. 'C'mon, Jaspa, you've got this.'

It all happens in less time than it takes to unzip a wetsuit. Jaspa is left looking down the line, stunned, watching Lisa tear apart the wave Jaspa should've been on. She glances over her shoulder to see Mel glaring at her.

'Jaspa, what the frick were you *thinking*?' Mel fumes, clenching her teeth and skimming the ocean with a closed fist. 'This is no time to play the nicey-pie samaritan!'

Jaspa stares at Mel like a naughty puppy caught doing the wrong thing. 'I've still got five minutes, I can do this, I promise.' She subtly shakes her head at herself, closes her eyes and looks away from her best friend. Jaspa's pretty sure she's blown it. Why does her heart always pull rank over her head, especially today of all days?

Two minutes pass and the ocean is flattened by the biggest lull they've seen all final. No one is catching any waves, meaning the positions remain the same. Three big droplets pound onto the deck of Jaspa's surfboard. She looks up and is surprised to see a thick blanket of rain. Pellets of water start pelting against her face, and a storm cloud hovers over them like a lump of charcoal.

The sudden darkness makes it difficult to decipher any movement in the ocean, and the loudness of the downpour slapping against the sea makes it impossible to know if the score for Lisa's ride has been announced yet.

Jaspa holds her watch a few centimetres from her face and notes that there are forty seconds remaining. She swallows back a gulp of tears as she realises she won't be joining her two best friends on the World Junior Tour next year.

As she anticipates the siren that will mark the end of the heat and braces herself for the questions she'll have to answer, she catches a glimpse of Mel paddling furiously to the outside of her, screaming, 'Go, just *GO!*'

A bit of swell bumps up underneath Jaspa, so she quickly strokes into position and takes the drop. The wave doesn't have the potential to be a heat winner; surely Mel knows that? But Jaspa figures at least she can have fun, go ballistic and surf it the best she ever has. She mightn't have made the tour, but no one can take surfing away from her.

Soaring into a turn at the base of the wave, before Jaspa even has the chance to transition her board, she sees Mel do the absolute unthinkable.

Five metres in front, Mel drops in on Jaspa, the worst sin you can commit in the competition. Right at that moment the rain lightens, and a stunned silence embraces the crowd as they see what's unfolding before them. It feels like the world has stopped around her as Jaspa stands, lifeless, like a mannequin glued to her surfboard, staring at Mel in disbelief. The wave shuts down and both surfers lie on their boards to ride the whitewater towards shore as the horn blasts and the red flag is raised. The final is over.

'Are you crazy? Mel, why did you just do that?' Jaspa cries as they glide within shouting distance. 'I do *not* want to be responsible for blowing your chances.'

'Well, you left me no friggin' choice did you? I was your only hope. I had a decision to make and I made it, so shut the hell up. I'm sick of your whining.' Mel uses her hand as a rudder to guide herself away.

A bump of backwash travels towards Jaspa. She lifts the nose of her board to hop over it, leans her elbow onto the deck and rests her forehead in her hand as she tries desperately to do the maths. Clearly, Mel used an interference so she'd be penalised her highest scoring ride, surrendering first place to Jaspa. But that means Pepita will move into second place. So where does that leave Mel? She needs to come third to qualify, but they're yet to hear the score of Lisa's ride. The very one Jaspa gave away to her. *Oh no, no, no, this can't be happening.*

Jaspa squeezes her thumb and forefinger deep into her temples. She's come around to the idea of being on the tour, but not without her best friend, and certainly not at the expense of her best friend's dream. The weight of worry bears down on her like a river of concrete. Sliding off her board, fatigued and helpless, she wades in the shallows, her legs wobbling. Mel's icy stare pierces Jaspa's heart and she wrestles with the notion of her best friend, who loves her so much, hating on her. She ignores her board flipping about in the shore break, the leg-rope still attached to her ankle, unable to muster the energy to unleash it. If Mel doesn't make it through, she'll never forgive herself. And she knows Mel won't, either. Jaspa's face screws up and her shoulders convulse as the sobs shoot out of her like cannonballs.

The commentary team builds the suspense, keeping everyone on standby as they wait for the official scores, notably Lisa's. Meanwhile, the men's final has been running for five minutes, but the drama of the women's showdown is capturing everyone's attention.

'Alright, here we have it.' The speakers silence the crowd.

Jaspa looks through watery eyes over at Mel, who stands dead still, her head hanging low.

'Lisa Campbell fourth on 8.1, Melissa Appleby third on 8.3, Pepita Mapstone second on 15.4 and Jaspa Ryder, congratulations, you are the Wiloonga Junior champion on 16.5.'

Jaspa runs through the rain to Mel, who collapses into a squat and drops her head, crying into her folded arms.

'Mel, we did it. We're through,' Jaspa weeps. She

knows Mel is going to be crazy angry, but the end result is perfect, and isn't that the main thing? 'I'm so sorry for what I did back there. You know I often do dumb stuff that makes no sense … I'm just really, really sorry,' Jaspa wails over the strengthening downpour.

Anger rises from Mel like a pitching wave. She stands and wipes her nose on her forearm. 'Jazz, you can't do that crap anymore, ya hear? This is serious. I can't … I *won't* look out for you like that when we're on tour,' she screams, making Jaspa flinch.

Jaspa buries her face in her hands. 'I know that, Mel,' she mumbles. 'I just felt sorry for Lisa and made a stupid decision.' She so badly wants to wrap her arms around Mel, to remind her that their friendship is what matters, but she'd feel less scared doing that to a great white shark at this moment.

An expression of annoyance creeps over Mel's face. 'Dammit. Lisa is a big girl, she can look after herself. Do you think she would've done the same for you? Do you? DO YOU?' She shoves Jaspa so hard she falls back onto the sand.

'Ow!' Jaspa winces. She looks up at Mel through blurry eyes, her bottom lip quivering, unable to speak. As her chest heaves with sobs, Jaspa wonders: *is this what it's like to be a professional surfer?*

Their families run across the sand through the driving rain, soaking wet and echoing a symphony of hoots and whistles, oblivious to the building tension between the girls. Their dads hoist them onto their shoulders and carry them into the well-wishing crowd surrounding the podium. No one notices that the two best friends are refusing to even make eye contact.

Jaspa climbs the stairs to the stage behind Mel, who stands in third place next to Pepita. As an official ushers Jaspa to the opposite side, she looks down to see Carolyn in the front row giving her a shaka sign. She grins and wriggles her fingers hello, wondering if Carolyn's even aware of the soap opera moments that just filled the final. Probably. Anyone close to Mel knows she never takes the easy route. Drama follows her around like that friend your parents warn you about but who you can't agree to let go of, because they're so *exciting*.

The countdown to the end of the boys' final can be heard, and Cooper is announced victorious on 16.5; the exact same score Jaspa secured her win with. Eva Hurst steps to the front of the stage carrying a microphone, wearing a spearmint hooded jersey dress and white Dunlop Volleys. She was a pro surfer on the main world tour, but after not qualifying for the last few years she's instead taken up TV presenting on *Wired*, a new TV channel solely dedicated to action sports.

Eva rambles off thanks to the long list of sponsors, and starts the congratulatory ceremony from fourth place, but Lisa isn't there. Rumour has it she split immediately after the final and started hitching back to Jan Juc.

Jaspa watches Mel collect her prize, but quickly drops her gaze when she swings around to get back in line. Right now, Jaspa wishes she could leap off this stage and run as far as her legs will carry her. The last thing she wants to do is give a speech and act all happy, considering what she's lost to get here. She glances up to silent stares from the crowd below and sees Eva waving her over with a laugh.

'Oops, sorry, I didn't hear you,' Jaspa whispers as she stands next to Eva and accepts her first-place trophy; a quirky surfer doll made from scraps of metal. Eva informs the crowd that Jaspa has also won a family holiday to Uluwatu Luxury Surf Villas in Bali, a Nikon waterproof camera, a $500 SurfStuff.com voucher and an Ocean Organics skincare basket. With a forced smile, Jaspa takes the microphone. What's she going to say? *Oh, thanks for these amazing prizes, but I don't deserve them.* Instead she figures she may as well use this opportunity to try and make amends.

Bringing the microphone to her lips, she looks over the mass of heads to focus on the ocean, willing her voice not to crack. 'Umm, hi. Um … I'd like to thank the contest organisers, Mum and Dad and Carolyn for their support, Aqua Adore for my free swimmers, and my best friend, Mel, for pushing me to be the best I can be – if it wasn't for her I wouldn't be here today.' She pauses to take in the rows of faces beaming up at her, searching for one person in particular. 'Lastly, I want to dedicate this win to my incredibly talented brother, Tyler Ryder.'

Who's nowhere to be seen.

#21

'Yo,' Carolyn demands with a clap of her hands, 'let's do this.'

Jaspa nods nervously, then links arms with Carolyn to walk up Whaler Road. Mel took the piece of paper, so they don't know the exact address, but it's not difficult to guess where the party's at. A deep bass beat thumps beneath their feet, and squeals and laughter can be heard a few houses away. Jaspa is taking ridiculously small baby steps, suddenly overwhelmed by a big dose of the jitters.

'It's gonna be fine, stop stressing,' Carolyn reassures her, lengthening her stride and pulling at Jaspa's locked elbow.

Jaspa contorts her mouth to one side into a grimace. She could definitely think of more enjoyable things to do than walking into a party where at least three of the people there are annoyed with her. 'Does Mel even know I'm coming?' she asks. Until now, Jaspa has avoided talking to Carolyn about the beach spat because she doesn't want to drag her off the fence and into the middle of it.

'Yep. And I'm sure she woulda come in with us —' Carolyn pauses, grappling for an excuse. 'But, you know, her place is in the opposite direction, so it was just easier for her to meet us there.'

'Uh huh, right.' That would be a fair assumption if they weren't talking about Mel — it takes a crowbar to release the grudges she holds. Jaspa stares at the driveway, knowing the best way is to make it quick, like ripping off a Band-Aid, rather than hovering uncomfortably at the entrance.

A skateboard ramp has been erected in the front yard, and a bunch of girls and guys, mostly dressed in black, are taking turns to outdo each other's tricks.

The back of the house is furnished with old couches and beanbags. A DJ up in the Rocket Fuel booth spins records, not paying much attention to the spread of girls loitering around, though it's clear they're not there for a song request. At a guess, there's at least fifty people scattered around, and the sun hasn't even set yet. This party is going to *pump*!

Jaspa and Carolyn scout around for a good position; somewhere with maximum people-watching potential. Jaspa's main requirement is that they're well away from

Tyler, who's slumped in a corner and has apparently been drowning his self-pity here since this afternoon. The friendly waitress from the cafe is straddled across him, using all her tricks to help him forget about his woes.

Just as they make a beeline for the empty sofa by the back fence, a voice pops up behind them. 'Hey, glad you made it.'

Jaspa swings around to see Kazumi Hall grinning at them. He cups his hands and shouts across the yard, 'Hey Mel! Your friends are here.'

Mel looks up, expressionless, pausing for a moment, then bounds her way over.

Jaspa glances at Carolyn, puzzled by Mel's enthusiasm.

'So, hot-shot, congrats, I hear you were a winner today,' Kazumi says to Jaspa innocently, unaware he could be dousing her with gasoline.

'Oh, umm, yes, thanks, thank you,' she says quickly as Mel approaches.

Mel launches herself between Jaspa and Carolyn and locks her arms around them. 'My chicks! I'm so glad you're here, I've missed you!' She smothers them with exaggerated kisses over their cheeks while Kazumi watches on, oblivious to the Oscar-worthy performance that's unfolding before him.

Jaspa stiffens suspiciously. 'I've … missed you too, Mel,' she draws out slowly. Surely Mel's not going to let her off that easily? She once gave Jaspa the silent treatment for days over not wanting to watch the same movie as her.

Mel leans in close to Jaspa. 'I'm still mad. We'll discuss later,' she whispers, then breaks away and sidles up next to Kazumi.

A little trickle of dread climbs up from Jaspa's stomach into her chest. Can't they just hug it out now, sincerely, and then move on and not look back? Mel almost thrives on drawing out conflict – Jaspa doesn't understand why. But she knows they'll still be best friends, so she may as well just enjoy the party.

Kazumi drapes his arm around Mel's shoulder, his fingertips nestling on the base of her neck. He draws her in close so the top of her head is pressed against his lips and whispers into her hair, 'Let's go for a walk, beautiful.'

She smiles and turns to meet his eyes, nodding. 'Yes please,' she says huskily.

'We're, umm, going to hang,' Mel says, glancing back over her shoulder and giving them a look that says, *I'm about to gather some serious gossip fodder, girls, so stay tuned!*

Jaspa watches Mel walk off and notices metaphorical daggers flying towards her from every other female in viewing distance.

'She's nothin' but trouble, that girl,' Carolyn teases as they head for the sofa.

'Yep, and that's why we love her,' Jaspa chimes as

they sit down to enjoy an unobstructed view of the shenanigans. Lochlan Jacobs, who is in their year at school, is throwing up in a garbage bin as his friends film him on their phones. The guys who heckled them on the beach yesterday take turns back-flipping off the fence. The Rocket Fuel promo girls prance around handing out free drinks, their shorts riding up so far they may cause permanent erosion.

'Look at those boobs – man, they'd make perfect tray tables,' laughs Carolyn.

Jaspa giggles at the promo girls sticking their chests out, wearing very low-cut tank tops and very high bras. 'I dare you to test them out – go and put a drink on them,' Jaspa says in hysterics.

'Well, I double D dare you!' Carolyn cracks up, before her expression changes and she nudges Jaspa with her elbow. 'Hey, Cooper's over there. What happened between you two anyway?'

Just like in the movies, everything around Jaspa seems to stop as her gaze pans around the room, zooming in on Cooper, who's leaning on the kitchen bench chatting to a couple of girls – thankfully without much interest, it seems.

'Dude, hello, what happened?' Carolyn repeats, knocking Jaspa's knee with hers.

'Oh, sorry. Well, did you see when I went to talk to him on the beach after my heat?'

Carolyn frowns and cocks her head. 'No, what happened?'

'Well, I was planning to do what you suggested and maybe let him know I like him, but he totally brushed me.' After finally talking about it, Jaspa notices the pain is a little less now. More like a butter knife in the heart than a dagger.

'Serious? Are you sure? Maybe he was just psyched to surf,' Carolyn suggests with a shrug.

Jaspa shakes her head and stares towards him. 'Nup, he snapped at me and made me feel about this big.' She holds her thumb and forefinger an inch apart. 'I thought he was different to most guys. The stupid thing is, I think I still really like him.'

Cooper meets Jaspa's gaze across the yard, and her cheeks flush the same shade as her pink dress.

'Urgh, this is torture,' Cooper mumbles to himself. His train of thought is derailed as a gorgeous brunette saunters up to him. She boldly slings her arms around his neck and murmurs, 'Congratulations, surfer guy,' into his ear, allowing her lips to brush against his lobe. Leaning her hips into his body she finds the contour of his mouth with hers, guiding him into a deep kiss. He pulls her closer towards him, circling his tongue lightly around hers.

Jaspa's jaw drops in disbelief. 'What an absolute rat,' she says, picking up her cup and swigging down her drink without taking a breath. Carolyn grabs Jaspa's arm and pulls her up off the couch.

'C'mon, let's go and look for some fun to get into.'

'That's a fabulous idea. I am *so* over wallowing.'

They walk across the makeshift dance floor, where a few guys are having a hip-hop battle. Carolyn drop-knees to the ground without warning and busts out the six-step, followed by a baby freeze. The guys pulse on the spot and hand jive to egg her on. She flips her palms backwards either side of her head and pushes to spring up onto her feet, then flicks her fingers at the B-boys and saunters away. Jaspa catches up to her and grabs her shoulders, laughing. They're headed for the skate ramp at the front of the house when a hand catches Jaspa's wrist.

'Hey, hi Jaspa.' An unfamiliar face beckons her closer.

'Sorry, do I know you?' she asks, hesitating. He's wearing a contest T-shirt, but she can't recall seeing him at any of the competitions.

'No, I don't think we've officially met yet. I'm Duncan Riley, the event's intern.'

Jaspa nods slowly. She remembers emailing Duncan a few weeks ago to register. 'Oh, Duncan, nice to put a name to a face. Oops, I mean a face to …'

He cuts in with a laugh before she has time to correct herself. 'You are unbelievable,' he whispers.

Jaspa notices Carolyn hovering uncomfortably next to them. 'Oh, sorry, Duncan this is Carolyn Fitzgerald.'

Carolyn offers a backwards nod hello but knows when she's at risk of rolling in as a third wheel. 'Yo, I'm gonna go skate, I'll see you in a bit.'

'No, no don't g–' Jaspa begins to protest, but Carolyn is already out of sight. She turns to face Duncan, offering an awkward smile and feeling a bit weird hanging out with this guy she's known for less than five minutes.

'Want to sit over there and chill? I'd love to get to know you,' he suggests, pointing to the couch the girls have just vacated.

'Umm, sure, why not?' she says reluctantly, knowing she'll once again have a front-on view of Cooper devouring the other girl. It might only be a butter knife, but it suddenly starts twisting and turning. How is she ever going to get a serious boyfriend if guys are going to be so confusing?

She spies Cooper looking at her out of the corner of his eye while he's still locking lips with the brunette. Before Jaspa even has time to think about what she's doing, she grabs the front of Duncan's shirt and opens her mouth onto his. Focused solely on whether Cooper can see her, Jaspa rides out the passionless kiss like a mushy wave, going through the motions and making it look way better than it actually is. Duncan moves his mouth too fast, and his tongue is like a soaking-wet towel. If she doesn't stop him soon, she's scared he'll swallow her whole face.

She pulls away and shakes her head. 'I'm sorry, I can't …' Springing up from the sofa to run and find Carolyn, she literally bumps into Mel. The words blurt out like water busting from a dam. 'Look, I love you. I'm really sorry I put you in that position, but I think everything turned out the way it should be and I really wish you weren't angry at me because Tyler hates me and Cooper's hooking up with a girl right in front of me and …' Jaspa draws in an exhausted breath and wipes the wetness from her face.

'Hey, hey, slow down.' Mel places both hands on Jaspa's shoulders and gives them a gentle shake. 'Look, I know I've been a brat – I was just mega-peeved at you for giving Lisa that wave. Let's put it behind us and celebrate instead.' Mel draws Jaspa in for a hug, then pulls back. 'And what the hell was that about Cooper?'

Jaspa sniffs and points towards the PDA.

'Urgh, boys … they just suck ass,' Mel says, putting on a brave face, even though her own eyes are glistening with emotion.

A look of confusion creeps onto Jaspa's face. She's been so concerned with her own woes, she didn't stop to think about what Mel's been doing for the last two hours. 'Why, Mel, what happened to you? Where's Kazumi?'

'Well, we hung out and mucked around, but then I

went to the bathroom, and when I came out I saw him walking off with some other chick.'

'Oh my god, that's awful! Come on, let's get out of here.' Jaspa swings her arm around Mel and they walk down the path to collect Carolyn.

'I'm almost thinking we make a no-dudes pact when we're on tour next year,' Mel says.

'Totally. I'm in if you are.'

Jaspa and Mel shake on what will absolutely be a broken promise.

#22

Two pieces of pumpkin seed bread pop out of the toaster. Jaspa collects them and immediately flings them onto the bench – they're hotter than expected. After sucking her fingers for relief, she smears on some avocado and miso paste, then squeezes a dribble of juice from a fresh lemon, which sprays onto her clean uniform. 'Urgh, I'm such a klutz,' she mutters while wiping herself with a cloth, not noticing Mel walk through the front door waving something in her hand.

'We're front-page news!' Mel holds up the local paper. A photo of the three of them sharing a wave spans the entire cover. In big bold font the headline reads: The Bikini Collective Slam Sexism!

'Oh my gosh, bring it here, bring it here!' Jaspa pleads, crunching into her breakfast.

Mel places the paper on the bench and opens it to

the double-page feature, which includes an article based on the interview, plus the letter they wrote to *Salt Action*. Jaspa points to a feature quote splashed across the centre: 'We believe female surfing is of interest to the entire surfing community, including guys.'

'Wow, they're your words, for the world to see!' Jaspa hopes this will divert Mel's attention from the obvious inclusion of – along with the beach photos that were taken by Sean – an extra one of Jaspa accepting her first-place trophy. Leaning back to rest on the bar stool, Jaspa admires an amazing image of Trudy Hardwick popping a huge grab-rail air. 'Oh wow, I can't believe they interviewed Trudy, too – this is massive!' she squeals.

'Read this part here for a bit of humble-pie eating,' Mel says, pointing to the end of the article.

Jaspa reads a quote from the editor of *Salt Action*, claiming he will now make a more conscious effort to consider female surfing content when planning their issues. To the side is a panel with some comments from the Facebook feed, plus stats on how many shares it received. Jaspa looks up at Mel, wide-eyed.

'I know, right,' Mel says, swiping Jaspa's last corner of toast. 'Can you believe the post has reached *eight thousand* likes already?'

'Mum, look, look!' Jaspa ambushes Ellen as she walks into the kitchen.

'Oh, what a wonderful photo, that's amazing. I'm

going to ask Josephine for a colour copy, I'd love to get it framed.' Ellen hands the paper back to Jaspa. 'You should take this to school just so they're across the media you're doing, although I'm sure they've already seen it. Do you need a lift?'

'No …' Jaspa starts to say, then looks out the window at the driveway. 'Oh, maybe. I thought Tyler would take us as usual, but the car's not there.' Jaspa has barely seen Tyler since she won the contest, apart from at the party. She later heard he'd had a massive blow-up with Cooper, and they ended up scuffling into the DJ booth and getting booted out. He caught a ride home with one of his friends the next day, and came in late last night to grab the spare car.

'Thanks for saving us from school bus torture, Mrs Ryder,' Mel deadpans as they pull out of the driveway. Jaspa peers through the car window at the mess of ocean. A storm hit in the early hours, carrying a huge swell and a rugged easterly wind. After seeing the forecast, Jaspa had texted Mel suggesting they reward themselves for their weekend's hard work with a sleep-in. Mel agreed, but insisted that first thing tomorrow they get back on the training program.

'If you see Tyler can you ask him to call home, just to check in?' Ellen asks as Jaspa gets out of the car.

'Sure, Mum. But you know he probably won't be at school today.' Jaspa kisses her mum on the cheek through the window.

'I know, honey. I'll pick you girls up this afternoon. Enjoy all the glory you'll get today.'

* * *

Jaspa waits at the side of the stage in the Institute's assembly hall. The sound of 500 students all trying to talk over each other bounces off the walls. In a school housing top athletes of all persuasions, everything is a competition, even the desire to be heard. She spies Mel and Carolyn sitting in the front row as promised and waves, trying to get their attention. But they're too engrossed in conversation to notice, and their laughter contributes to the building wall of sound.

Jaspa reaches back and runs a finger along the outline of her Bonds boylegs, checking that none of her school uniform has crept into places it shouldn't. Just as she gives herself the all-clear, she senses someone standing behind her. Whipping her head around, slightly startled, she finds herself face to face with Cooper. Her mouth drops open but no words come to mind, so she just stands there looking like a possum frozen in headlights.

Cooper smiles and melts the ice away, but although Jaspa's not the best at people reading, she's pretty sure there's none of the flirtatious flavour he sprinkled her with at dinner the other night.

'Hi, Jaspa. Hey, well done on the weekend, I hear

you surfed really well.' His head is angled down, but he peers at her from beneath his hair. Oh, goodness, how she wants to grab his school shirt and slide her lips into his parted mouth and just freeze there for a moment.

'Thanks, I, umm, I hear you did, too,' she stumbles. 'I mean, I didn't hear you surfed well but I'm assuming you did cos you won.' The puzzled look on Jaspa's face makes it clear that even she doesn't know why she just said that. Geez, why couldn't she just say she saw him surf, like a normal, fumble-free person would?

Jaspa is saved by Principal Mackerel, who calls their names and ushers them onto the stage. He announces their competition wins from the weekend, hands them each a bouquet of native flowers and encourages the students to give them a round of applause. Jaspa brings her bouquet up to her nose to avoid looking at the sea of people in front of her and breathes in its woody scent. These ceremonies are a regular fixture at the Institute, but Jaspa's usually the one looking up at the recipient. The principal then goes on to congratulate the other students, Mel, Carolyn, Ryan Thompson and Vijay Kumar on qualifying for the World Junior Tour.

Mel blows Jaspa a kiss from her seat and Carolyn gives her two thumbs up. Jaspa smiles and wonders what it will be like a year from now, when they've been travelling the world as competitive surfers. As she swivels to exit the stage, a guy bellows from the back of the room, 'Show us ya bikini collective!' Spot fires of snickers ignite around the room, so Jaspa walks briskly towards the stairs.

Mel seizes the opportunity to douse the flames by leaning back in her chair, cupping her hands around her mouth and throwing her voice to the ceiling. 'In your dreams, loser.'

'Alright, alright, that's enough,' Mr Mackerel says over the eruption of laughter. 'Assembly dismissed, time for your classes. And quietly.'

Jaspa meets Mel and Carolyn outside and they make their way along the cobblestone path towards C block for their surfing theory lesson.

'I guess everyone read the paper, then,' Jaspa says, stuffing the bouquet into her calico tote.

'Don't worry about it, it's a good thing. That was just Troy Brody being a smartarse,' Mel says, hopping onto each raised rock in the path the way you have to when jumping off Bonita Point. 'He's probably just jaded cos he's pretty much lost every tennis match this year. He may even be booted.'

Cutting across the courtyard, the three of them are intercepted by Vera Lee and Susan Riley from the swimming team.

'Well done on your letter to *Salt Action*, girls. That article in the paper is killer,' says Vera, with her arms folded around her notebook.

Susan squints, shading her eyes from the sun with her forearm. Jaspa notices a band of muscle running from her elbow to her wrist like a taught rubber band. The swimmers train harder than almost anyone else at the school. Earlier, too. The thought of rising at five every morning seems as much of a chore to Jaspa as an end-of-year essay. Funnily, she sees getting up for a sunrise surf as totally different.

'That bit you said about standing up for yourself, I so hear you,' Susan adds. 'The amount of times guys target me out there because they know they can scab waves off me …'

'Well, remember, don't let them hassle you,' Mel cuts in, playfully pretending to box at the air. 'Paddle strong and just go for it. If you make it, you make it, if you don't, you don't. No matter.'

'Hey, you girls should come down to surf Bonita with us sometime,' Jaspa offers. There's nothing more fun than a massive girl surfing posse. In fact, what better way to give voice to their cause than with as many girls as possible? She tugs at Mel's arm and whispers, 'Hey, I've got an idea.'

'Oh goodie,' Mel claps. 'You're finally going to agree to cut class and come shopping with me in Byron Bay?'

Jaspa rolls her eyes. 'No, smarty. Come on, I'll tell you.' She says goodbye to Susan and Vera and links arms with Mel and Carolyn, guiding them to a patch of grass outside their classroom.

'Okay, master plan, spill,' Mel says, flopping on the ground and leaning her chin in her hand.

Jaspa taps on her phone screen and holds it in front of her. 'Remember this thing that came out a few years ago, the Right 2 Be Me page?'

'Oh yeah,' Carolyn clicks her fingers and points. 'Wasn't that to rat out bullies?'

'Kind of,' Mel joins in, scrounging around the bottom of her bag for a mint. 'It was more a safe space for those being bullied, to talk about their feels.' She blows a piece of fluff off a Tic Tac then pops it in her mouth. 'What's that got to do with us?'

Jaspa puts down her phone and pulls her mane of hair over one shoulder. 'Susan and Vera got me thinking – there must be heaps of surfer girls everywhere who could do with some support and encouragement.' She pulls the newspaper out of her bag and throws it on the grass. 'If we're going to be a bikini collective, then surely the more …'

'… the merrier!' Springing to her knees, Mel cups Jaspa's shoulders. 'Oh my god, I love it! We can make it a closed group for chicks only.'

Jaspa coughs out a succession of laughs as Mel shakes her back and forth. 'And when we're travelling we can spread the word all over the world.' Jaspa is loving the idea of making being a pro surfer mean something more than just point tallies.

'No dudes?' Carolyn asks, screwing up her nose. 'Sounds snoring.'

'Carolyn!' Mel takes her hands off Jaspa and grabs Carolyn in a headlock. 'Don't worry, you're going to get a smorgasbord of boy candy on the tour,' she says, licking the side of Carolyn's face.

'Oh, you feral. Okay, okay, count me in.' Carolyn wrenches Mel's arm over her head and wipes her cheek with her uniform. 'But don't expect me to be a role model. I don't look like you two.'

Jaspa frowns. 'Carolyn, don't say that. It's not about that.' She hates how society is so focused on looks. Carolyn inspires her in so many ways. Her independence. The way she can nail any sport she tries. Her relationships with guys, who seem to scramble over themselves to befriend her. And the way she steamrolls through life despite never being given the easy road. Jaspa squeezes Carolyn's knee. 'In fact, let's make it the very opposite.' Jaspa fishes out her notebook and holds her pencil in the air. 'So, what else? What's our vision?'

'I agree, firstly it should be reassuring girls that it's not all about being blonde, blue-eyed and beautiful,' Mel says, pressing her index finger into the palm of her other hand to indicate a point, before backtracking. 'Sorry, no offence, Jaspa!'

'Well, that should be our first pact, then.' Jaspa scribbles in her notebook. 'Number one: we embrace everybody. Including blondes,' Jaspa adds with a smirk, flicking Mel with her pencil.

'Hey, that's kinda cool. Like, ev-er-y bo-dy,' Carolyn says, drawing out each syllable and slapping her hands from her bum down her thighs.

'Do you like this?' Mel asks, pointing to a photo of the three of them riding a wave, all flashing a peace sign. 'Should we make this the profile shot?'

'Oh, I love it,' Jaspa gasps. 'How did you get it?'

'I just texted Sean and asked if he had any spares from our photo shoot. He also gave us a bunch of other images we can use of waves and sunsets.'

'Can we pretty please add an inspirational quote to it?' Jaspa pleads with her hands clasped in front of her face. 'That one I love by Trudy Hardwick: "I'm not having fun because I'm the best, I'm the best because I'm having fun." We could even change it every week.'

'Alright, and we title the page The Bikini Collective?' Mel asks, typing it into the template.

'Yes!' Jaspa claps.

'Yeah, but what's it mean? Will everyone else get it?' Carolyn asks, scrunching up her nose.

Mel nods. 'Hey, good point. So something under it, like: We're female. We surf. Discuss.'

'Or: Surf like a girl and own it,' Carolyn clicks her fingers in the air.

Jaspa stares ahead and visualises herself riding a wave. Weaving up and down, smiling and laughing.

What makes them different to guy surfers? That's what they need to capture. Surfing grace? Eww, no, that's too whimsical. Surfer girls? Too done. 'Ooooh, I think I've got it!' Jaspa leans on all fours and shuffles in to close up the circle. 'What about: The Bikini Collective – a girl's-eye view of surfing.'

#23

Tyler gently pulls at his eyelashes and a crust crumbles between his thumb and forefinger. It could be the result of salt build-up from the howling onshore wind. Or, more likely, the fact that he has spent the last hour head down, bawling.

A balloon of breath gets caught in his chest and a multitude of thoughts tussle inside his head. What is he going to do? The surfing tour isn't just an entry in his life itinerary, it's the only thing on the list. He certainly isn't going to become his little sister's tour gopher, like Cooper sarcastically suggested in retaliation moments after Tyler smacked him unprovoked in the face. What else, then? A dishpig at Subway? Go to uni for four years? And while he's in Australia living out his lame-ass existence, doing nothing spectacular, his sister will be travelling the world. She'll get sponsored, probably win some events, become the tour's pin-up girl. The whole world is going to fall in love with her. There's only so much bitterness Tyler's stomach can handle before exploding.

He continues to stare out to sea. The wind whips aggressively against the board tucked under his arm, so he steadies himself and tightens his sweaty grip on the bottom rail. The ocean looks as mean as she gets. Today, she hasn't got one iota of mercy. Mountains of whitewater tear across the surface, clapping like thunder as the waves collide with rocks that protrude from the cliff like broken glass. Tyler jiggles up and down on his toes, looking north to see the faint outline of the Bonita Point headland that's blanketed behind a haze of salty air. He's craving the security of home while also feeling suffocated at the thought of returning. Tyler would normally only surf Kamikazes on a light offshore wind with swell half the size it is today – even then it lives up to its name. It's the most challenging wave on the east coast, and today it seems like a death wish.

Sea urchins sway in the surrounding rock pools, their flower-like beauty belying the pain they can cause. Tyler prepares to take a step then hesitates, wondering how he's even going to get 10 metres past the shore break, and whether he even really wants to. He could turn back now – no one would know. There's nothing he needs to prove. A fresh tear trickles from his eye and is whipped away by the easterly wind. Tyler picks up the slack of the leg-rope that's velcroed to his ankle and thinks, *stuff it*, hopping across the ledge and launching himself into the washing machine of water.

#24

The text on the screen behind Mr Sampson reads: *PRIORITY: what it is / how to get it / how to use it.* He has spent the morning explaining to the class that while they might use priority or 'right of wave' positioning as amateur competitors – much as you do when free-surfing your local break – once you hit the big league and qualify for the main professional tour they use a different ruling for their two-surfer heats. The primary advantage of this is that the surfer who gains priority can take any wave they want, regardless of their position in the take-off zone.

'How might you use this system to your advantage?' Mr Sampson asks the class, then points to Mel, who immediately raises her hand.

'If you're in the lead towards the final minutes of your heat, you can sit close to your competitor and block any heat-winning waves,' Mel answers, then sits back, ready to collect her praise.

'That's right, Mel. In fact, some of you might recall that's exactly how Kazumi Hall secured his world title last year,' Mr Sampson responds while typing Mel's answer onto the projected iPad.

Jaspa glances sideways at Mel, who narrows her eyes and scrunches her nose.

'Just pretend you didn't hear that,' Jaspa whispers, reaching around and placing her hands either side of Mel's head to cover her ears.

Mr Sampson explains how Kazumi played priority tactics in the final event at Pipeline by blocking his competitor from using any waves to take the lead. Instead, Kazumi coaxed him into a monster set the surfer was far too deep to make, and while his opponent was left to pick reef bits out of a torn butt cheek, Kazumi celebrated like the champion he is.

Two girls at the back of the class whisper to each other as the teacher notes more of the students' responses. The blonde leans in to her friend. 'Apparently she was trailing Kazumi Hall *everywhere* on the weekend, like a pathetic puppy dog,' she gossips, her eyes darting in Mel's direction. 'Right in front of his girlfriend.'

'You think that's lame, did you watch the final?' the other girl asks out the side of her mouth. 'Jaspa wouldn't have even made it on tour if it wasn't for her bosom buddy holding her hand.'

'I know, right ...' The blonde stops mid-sentence, realising Carolyn is within earshot and firing a round of filthy looks their way. These two have developed a reputation for being bitchy around the comps lately, talking up their surfing far beyond their capabilities.

'Do you have something to contribute, girls?' Mr Sampson interjects.

'No, sir,' they mumble, avoiding Carolyn's glare. Jaspa shoots Carolyn a questioning look, and she shakes her head and rolls her eyes.

Thomas claps his hands to regain the students' attention. 'Right up until the late nineties, the pro tour only used a priority buoy system.' He brings up a diagram of two squares representing surfers, a circle further out to sea marking the buoy, and two dotted loops showing the surfers' paddling path around the buoy. 'In order to gain priority, a competitor would need to be the first one to paddle around the buoy. Eventually this system changed for the two-surfer heats; can anyone tell me how?' A hand shoots up in the front row from a boy whose dead-straight sandy bob could see him star in *Dogtown and Z-Boys*.

'Dylan?'

'They started using jet skis?'

'Correct. Jet skis were introduced to transport surfers after they catch a wave. It's the same principle –

the first surfer to arrive out the back of the line-up is granted priority.' He pauses and points in the vicinity of the buoy on the screen. 'But why do you think the jet skis were even introduced if the intention is the same?' The class sits with a mix of blank, disinterested and thoughtful expressions.

'The buoy kept moving with the currents?' offers Jason Daniels, who's sitting next to Carolyn.

'No, but good answer. What do you think the main benefit of jet skis versus paddling would be?' The teacher waits with an eager expression.

'Less tiring for the competitors,' Jaspa pipes up, removing her hands from Mel's ears. She'd love to get carried into the line-up by a jet ski!

'Exactly!' he says with a pointing motion. 'And *why* would this be a good thing?'

'Because they would be less tired?' Jaspa answers slowly.

Mr Sampson swallows back a guffaw at Jaspa stating the obvious, then props himself against the corner of the desk. 'Yes … and being less tired means they can catch more waves, which would be good for …'

'Us, watching online,' Carolyn shouts without prompt. She doesn't have unlimited data at home, so streaming surfers paddling 200 metres around a buoy at a break like Bells would be as exciting as watching resin dry.

The teacher nods and goes on to explain the many

ways surfing has improved its format to be a spectator sport and why these changes were essential for commercial growth. Jaspa half-listens while replaying the assembly encounter with Cooper over in her mind. Maybe he *was* flirting and she just didn't read him right. Her head is locked in a stand-off with her heart, wondering why she's wasting her daydream hook-up scenarios on a guy who is clearly not interested. Her head says he's a douchebag, but her heart counters that he's just misunderstood. She begins scrawling two options on paper for how to solve the Cooper mystery when she hears her name being called. Jolting her head up to look at Mr Sampson, she's confused to see he's still posting notes on the projector. Mel gives her arm a gentle jab with her pen and points at the classroom door, where the school's receptionist is waving Jaspa over.

Oh, this can't be good. The last time she was called from class was when Grandpa Ryder died.

#25

Tyler clings to a rock and tries to ignore the excruciat-
ingly painful throb pulsating through his left ankle. The
cracking sound it made as he landed after freefalling
into his first wave – an ugly, mutated, ten-foot monster –
still rings in his ears, a sonic reminder of how much
trouble he's in right now. Surges of whitewater scrape
him across a reef shelf and into the ascending cliff. He
can't work out which pain is worse: the cramping in his
fingertips from clutching on for his life, which feels like
it's about to be washed away, or the gash on his thigh,
which opens further each time he's ripped across barna-
cles. Tyler knows he's done plenty of stupid things in his
life to fill up his cup of consequence, but this stunt has it
overflowing.

* * *

At the river-mouth entrance, one beach south of Bonita Shores, the bottom half of a snapped surfboard has become entangled in a fisherman's line. He reels it in and, being a local surfer, recognises it as Tyler's by the half-torn sponsors' stickers. He wouldn't normally be concerned. It isn't unusual to come across broken boards – they usually end up either dumped in beach bins or as ornaments in people's front yards. But today is different. The sea is savage, and a snapped surfboard could signal something very wrong.

Jaspa waits at the school gate, picking at her fingernails. She draws in a sharp breath as one rips so far down it pulsates and threatens to bleed. Shaking it doesn't help relieve the sting, so she sticks it in her mouth.

The receptionist's words play over in her mind. The fact that her brother is missing doesn't seem like such a big deal; he's a seventeen-year-old boy, and disappearing for a night and a day isn't out of the ordinary for Tyler. But the fact that her mum and dad are picking her up early from school is. They're not worrywarts.

She looks at her phone to see another text message from Mel. She replies:

Hey, they're still not here. I'll fill you in as soon as I know the deets. Love you xxx

Loose bits of gravel crack under the weight of the bulky Dunlop tyres as the family car comes to a halt in front of Jaspa. She climbs into the back and rests her hands on the driver and passenger seats, pulling herself forward.

'What's going on? I'm kinda freaking out,' she asks.

'Hopefully it's nothing, but Ned found Tyler's broken board while fishing, and the car's parked at Shellhaven,' Anthony replies, easing into first gear and driving towards the highway.

'What, no … he wouldn't have gone out at Kamikazes today, would he?' Jaspa flops back and clicks on her seatbelt. The only break any sane person would even consider surfing today would be kiddie corner at the Grove; it's the only place that would be remotely protected.

'We're really not sure,' Ellen says, her elbow propped against the window with her head resting in her hand. 'We need to find out.'

'I'm sure he's probably just ditched one of his old boards into the ocean to ask Huey for some waves,' Jaspa figures, referring to the old-school surfer ritual of sacrificing a busted surfboard by either burning it on the beach or throwing it into the sea as a prayer to the surf god for good swell. She's never done it herself, though – either approach would be awful for the environment.

'Possibly,' Ellen responds. 'Can you put something online, or anywhere you have the same friends, please?'

'Okay, sure, Mum.' She types a post:

Hey guys, if any of you have seen Tyler can you let me know asap? It's urgent!!

She tags eleven of their mutual friends, including Cooper, who she's never communicated with online until now. While she's at it, she snoops around on Cooper's page, checking for any trace of a female presence. A girl's gotta keep informed, after all.

Ellen answers her phone. 'Yes, yes, I understand,' she says over and over. Hanging up, she mumbles to Anthony, 'The police said not to panic just yet but to keep them updated.'

Jaspa hears her mum start to whisper to herself, begging for Tyler to please be safe. She reaches over the car seat and massages her shoulder. Jaspa doesn't share her mum's worry. He's probably off in one of his mates' cars somewhere, gone dirt biking or something.

The new Sandy Shores song comes on the radio. 'Dad, can you turn it up please?' Jaspa asks. She's loved the singing siblings ever since seeing them at a free beach concert for Sea Shepherd last year. She sings along to the reggae groove, hoping it will lighten the mood.

*I promise you in a moment I'll come
to meet you at the setting sun
with a hand on my heart you'll know for sure
my love for you won't come undone.'*

They're one of her dad's favourite bands, too. He relaxes his shoulders and taps his fingers to the beat on the steering wheel, giving Jaspa a smile and a wink in the rear-view mirror. Just as she's about to text Mel to let her know everything's probably going to be okay, that Tyler's gone AWOL but she's sure they'll find him soon, she spots a handful of responses to her post. Most of them are Tyler's mates being smartarses:

I hear he's still looking for his dummy at the contest site.

*He's teaching **Stanley Albert** how to finally do a cutback.*

More like he's teaching your mamma.

But it's the final comment, from Toby Lackey, that catches her eye:

He messaged me this morning to see if I wanted to go out at Kamas. Why?

26

Tyler runs his tongue across his lips. Instead of experiencing wet, silky relief from the dryness, it's like a scourer rubbing against sandpaper. He's never regretted a night of drinking more than he does right now. The couple of spews he's had have probably helped purge his hangover, but they've also fast-tracked the immense dehydration. Oh, the cruel irony; to be so parched while surrounded by water. His throat feels like a dried-up prune, and a throbbing starts knocking against the inside of his skull.

He opens his eyes briefly and the sun's rays pierce his eyeballs. Judging from its position, it must be past midday. He manages to angle his hand, without losing his grip, to see his watch: it's 1.50 pm. The tide has started to recede, and while the ocean is still creeping up to his waist, it's no longer surging over his head and ping-ponging him against the cliff. It's good to be grateful for the little things.

The closest thing he has to a plan for getting back to the beach is to wait and see if the swell subsides, then figure out how to make it to shore. The thing is, Kamikazes is not like your regular beach break. Even at low tide, the ocean meets the cliff around the entire bay. Equally challenging is that the shore isn't sand, it's a smothering of rocks. Getting in is twice as hard as the paddle out. With a mix of small round boulders and jagged obstacles of many lethal shapes and sizes, there's only one paddle-in spot free of anything that might rip out your fins or flesh. Straining his neck, Tyler looks up at the cluster of shrub growing from the cliff that he needs to line himself up with. It's hard enough negotiating this position on a surfboard and on a swell half this size, let alone swimming in the opposite direction, against the current, while tired, thirsty, hungry and in the most pain he's ever experienced. He pushes himself closer to the rock and grimaces. Even if he miraculously makes it to the track, how is he going to handle the trek up the cliff with a busted ankle?

Lethargy weighs down on him at the thought of moving anywhere. His eyes close as he makes three wishes: that someone's stupid enough to come out for a surf and spots him. That his parents realise he's missing and call the police. That he wasn't such a tool.

And then he passes out.

#27

Jaspa sets up a Facebook event titled Tyler Search Party, and types in 3.30 pm as the start time. She stares, blinking, at the spot for the finishing time and a coolness darts through her veins. There's no way she's leaving it blank. After a moment's thought, she enters 5 pm. That's a realistic compromise.

She sits on the end of her bed, unties the string of her notebook and rips out a piece of paper. In hurried scribble she writes an affirmation for Tyler and places it into her manifestation jar among the many bits of paper hosting her other hopes, such as passing exams, getting a tube for more than ten seconds and having Cooper fall in love with her. She'd give up all of them to have the wrath of her brother back in her presence right now.

She slumps, motionless, staring at the wall as her

mind tries to get a grip on the situation. Not knowing how this scenario is going to end, or even how it began, is poisoning her mind. *Where the heck is he?*

Visions of Tyler struggling in the ocean keep popping into her head, leaving her short of breath. She hyperventilates the sadness in and out, in and out. Closing her eyes, she sucks a trail of air in through her nostrils, deep into her stomach, and holds it. Fighting back tears, she lets out an audible sigh, shakes her shoulders and visualises her brother sitting right beside her. She's managed to suppress every urge to cry so far – surprising for someone who even blubbers during nature documentaries. But crying would mean admitting that something is wrong, and seeing her upset is the last thing her parents need right now. Her mum collapsed onto the couch, heaving with sobs, when they returned from their first search along the Shellhaven clifftop, and she's barely stopped crying since.

Jaspa shuffles down the stairs to offer her mum a cup of tea, only to see that she's fallen asleep. A sense of peace has momentarily erased the crease that has etched Ellen's brow since the moment she realised Tyler was missing. Jaspa wishes there was a way she could gather up all her mum's worries while she slept, so she could wake up happy.

'I've had over twenty people so far offer to come to help us look,' Jaspa tells her dad quietly, tiptoeing into the kitchen to fill up her water bottle.

Anthony offers her a pained smile. 'That's great, button. I think we'll leave your mum here to rest. I'm just writing her a note.'

'Have you talked to Grandma yet?' Jaspa asks, packing some apples and bananas into her backpack. Anthony's mum lives half the time at Bonita Shores, in their backyard garden flat, and the rest of the time at her sister's home on the Sunshine Coast. 'I miss her,' Jaspa says, picking up the soap from the sink and sniffing it, the lavender scent reminding her of Grandma Ryder. 'It feels like she's been gone forever.'

Anthony stands up from the table and scans the room for his car keys. 'Yep, I called her a little while ago. She's coming home tomorrow,' he replies absently.

Jaspa studies the dark rings drooping beneath his eyes, the sadness weighing them down. 'I guess we'd better get going huh, Dad?' she suggests softly.

He nods and creeps across the floor to kiss Ellen's forehead, then ushers Jaspa through the front door.

The mass of whitewash looks like a herd of wild white horses bucking on the ocean, making Jaspa shudder. She's not yet ready to accept that her brother might be out there somewhere. Tucking her legs underneath her in the front seat, she turns towards the driver's side. 'Dad, what exactly *is* our plan?'

Anthony takes his hand off the gearstick and ruffles her hair. 'Sergeant Moss has arranged the search parties and we're meeting our group back at Shellhaven cliff.'

'Do you really think he went surfing out there?' she asks, gripping onto the seat as the car winds around the continuous hairpin bends.

'Who knows, button,' he sighs, staring at the road behind his sunglasses. 'I really wish I knew.'

A haze of dust surrounds them as they bump along the dirt road leading to Kamikazes. Jaspa places her palm against the window and presses her nose to the glass in silence as they pass their spare car, still parked where Tyler left it.

'A few people are here already,' Jaspa mutters as they skid to a stop. She draws in a deep breath to prevent her heart from pounding right through her ribcage. Fifteen faces look in her direction and although she can't see behind their sunglasses, it's obvious they all share the same expression of pity. Jaspa stays close to her dad, hanging onto the side of his T-shirt for security like a toddler would, and scans the crowd for Mel. *Where on earth is she?*

'Good to see you, Anthony, Jaspa.' Sergeant Moss tips his hat and leans in to grip Anthony's hand in a firm handshake. 'We're just waiting for a few more volunteers and then we'll split into two search groups. Mary and Tony will scale the cliff,' he says, nodding his head towards two officers who are unravelling abseiling ropes.

'Where will we be loo–?' Jaspa croaks, not quite getting out the last word. She coughs into her hand.

'Excuse me … looking. Where will we be looking for my brother?'

Sergeant Moss points north. 'You and your father can join the team on Shellhaven beach.'

Jaspa nods, then turns to Anthony. 'I'll be back in just a sec, Dad.' She wanders over to the path that descends to the main beach and looks down at the stretch of sand that's becoming more exposed by the minute as the tide surges out to sea. A bubble of anxiety gets stuck in Jaspa's stomach. The ocean is at her most ferocious, the swell pitching powerful waves onto shallow waters, the crash as loud as a semi-trailer dumping a load of concrete. The beach is carpeted in brown foam and entire tree trunks have wedged themselves into exposed sandbanks. Jaspa gasps as she sees black dots scattered along the shore, birds that took a chance and flew too close to the water.

She swallows back her tears as she returns to Anthony's side. Feeling her phone buzz in her pocket, she pulls it out and sees a text from Carolyn.

'Dad, Carolyn says sorry she can't come, she has to work and can't get a lift in time.' Jaspa shoves the phone back into her pocket. 'Have you seen Mel yet?' she sighs.

As Anthony shakes his head, she spies a group of five people walking towards them, two in Institute school uniforms. As they draw near, Jaspa realises one of them is Mel. But what is she *doing* with Cooper?

28

Tyler lies semi-conscious in the cave. Just before passing out again, he managed to pull himself behind a bigger rock into a slightly sunken alcove. It's offered some protection from the pounding waves and blistering sun, giving him a chance to rest. In the moments he's been awake, Tyler has thought mostly about his family. He half hopes they've noticed him missing so they can send help, but also wonders if it's better they don't know, so his mum doesn't go nuts with worry. That way he can get himself to shore, rock up at home and it'll all be sweet, with plenty of stories to tell over Christmas lunch.

The scrapes along his thigh throb like a dubstep drop. He looks down at the custard-like layering and touches the surrounding ring of inflamed red, sucking in a sharp breath. The last reef cut he endured was on a surfing trip in the Mentawais. His treatment was at the hands of three merciless friends: one to hold him down, one to scrape a scourer over the cut then squeeze in the lime juice, and one to film it. In that moment he hated them with vitriol, but their quick thinking meant he was back in the water the next day. Now, he'll probably be lucky to keep the limb.

Suddenly Tyler is jolted out of his thoughts. Are those *voices*? He could be tripping out, but he's pretty sure he just heard people shouting. He eagerly props himself up, leaning against his hands and trying to zone out the thumping noise of the ocean.

He holds his breath and listens.

Listens.

Listens.

There it is! Someone – people – are definitely nearby. And what's that shuddering above him? A chopper? It is, it's a freakin' helicopter. He gets a flip of excitement in his stomach and grins for the first time in at least eighty hours, since before he lost at the contest.

A male voice bellows out his name and he screams in response, 'I'm here. I'm down here!' But nothing releases from his voicebox beyond a weak crackle. He tries again, summoning the sound from the depths of his stomach.

Nothing.

The helicopter continues to circle above, but he's hidden behind the stupid rock that was supposed to save his life. Maybe he should drag himself back off the reef ledge and into the ocean in the hope that someone might see him? But that's a stupid idea, right? His instincts are giving him nothing. He has no idea what to do.

Cooper and three friends are searching the base of the cliff track at the Kamikazes jump-off spot. But the waves spraying up against them make it hard to get close. Their group's leader has shouted at them several times to get the hell away from the area, but they ignore him.

'Dude, how would he have even planned to paddle in, it's a junkyard out there,' says Jeremy Weeks, unzipping his fly and taking a leak.

'Jesus, put that away,' Cooper says, shoving him in the chest. 'There are cops everywhere, you're a bloody idiot.'

Cooper stares out to sea as his friends start the trek back up the trail. He watches the powerful lines of swell march in from the open ocean, pitch up and throw themselves towards shore. Cooper guesses some of the waves are at least 10 feet – it's difficult to tell, but the low tide surges mean they're far from anything you would want to try and surf. They move in dangerous, mesmerisingly beautiful slow motion. Cooper hopes that if he concentrates hard enough, Tyler will suddenly appear. He may've been a tool lately, but he's still his best mate.

Regret continues to torment Cooper. He should have been more compassionate and supportive. If *he* was the one who hadn't qualified for the tour he'd have been gutted, too. Tyler's definitely not the most gracious of losers, but he's not the sorest Cooper has encountered, either.

He cups his hands over his mouth and hollers Tyler's name, heaving his chest to throw his voice as far as he can, but the onshore easterly cruelly throws it back towards him. He wipes the wetness from his face, his sadness flowing like a tap on full, and turns with a sigh to return to the car park. If he had just loitered a little longer, looked north towards the headland and focused his gaze underneath the hanging cliff, he just might've seen an arm waving frantically at him from behind a large triangular rock.

#29

Jaspa wakes to find herself sobbing. Mel is contoured behind her with an arm draped over Jaspa's chest. The best thing about spooning is you can draw on the other person's emotional support without having to look them in the eye. She can feel Mel's face nuzzled into the base of her neck. It feels damp. Mel sniffles quietly. 'Do you want a tissue?' Jaspa asks into the pillow.

Mel's not usually a crier. Well, she's not usually a *subtle* crier. Her tears are more likely to flow in fits of passion, exploding after being wound up like a jack-in-the-box. 'No thanks, I'll just keep using your shirt,' Mel smirks, blowing Jaspa's hair away from her mouth.

Through the sheer bedroom curtains, wisps of purple scatter across the sky like marble. Jaspa's pained by the beauty of the sunset, which triggers a hopeless desperation within everyone she knows as they settle in to endure nine hours of darkness, hoping Tyler is some-where safe, sleeping. Her gaze travels towards the small television she'd moved from the study.

'Do you want me to turn that off?' Mel asks as yet another news report appears on the screen.

Jaspa shakes her head, reaches for the remote and turns up the volume. A reporter stands on the clifftop at Shellhaven beside the 'Hazard: dangerous surf' sign that has been ignored by many a surfer. Wind whips her perfectly styled hair in every direction as she speculates on the reason for Tyler's 'daredevil act'. Stupidity? Angst? Adrenaline? The broadcast cuts away to footage of waves thumping into the rocks with inset shots of Tyler throwing his board after losing the competition, and another of him taken at Easter, a surfboard under his arm, his face covered in white zinc, smiling straight at the camera. It's the face of someone whose story has now caught the attention of the entire nation.

'Oh, Daddy,' Jaspa whispers as Anthony appears on the TV, squinting against the wind and pleading for everyone to keep their eyes peeled, insisting that he believes Tyler will be found.

'No way, what's this? Turn it up,' Mel urges when a picture of B-grade celebrity Tom Tansy, who plays the part of a surf hippie in locally filmed soapie *Pacific Dreams*, flashes on the screen. The report explains that Tom has shared the Find Tyler Ryder Facebook page with his fans, helping it reach 20,000 shares in under an hour.

Jaspa turns off the television and throws the remote onto the end of the bed. 'You know what the weird thing is?' she asks Mel rhetorically, running her thumb over her friend's fingernail. 'I don't even know how I should be feeling right now. Should I be happy because in my heart I know we're going to find him? And am I delusional to even believe that? Should I be grieving right now?' She rolls onto her back, arching it so Mel can pull her arm out from underneath. Jaspa's insides keep threatening to hurl up the contents of her stomach. She now realises the term 'sick with worry' is an actual thing, not just an exaggeration mothers throw around to guilt-trip you.

'Jazz, I feel pretty helpless, and it's eating at me,' Mel says, both of them staring up at the ceiling. 'I'm such a control freak. I can't handle not being able to steer a situation in the direction I want it to go, or to at least find a solution.'

Jaspa turns towards Mel and forces a grin. 'Well, one of us has to be like that, otherwise we'd never get anything done. You know how bad I am at making decisions.'

'True,' Mel agrees with a whisper. 'And you know how bad I am at accepting other people's.'

They lie in silent stillness for a while, their thoughts hovering above them. Jaspa doesn't need to kid herself.

She knows very well why Tyler's been so harsh on her the past couple of years. When Jaspa inherited his old banged-up board, the last thing he expected was that she'd go on to be a more successful surfer than him. All those industry eyes that are on her should be on him. That's probably one reason she's so nonchalant about *trying* to be one of the best; she doesn't want to rub his nose in it. She makes a silent promise that if Tyler doesn't want her to go on the world tour, she won't. In the brief moment between her win and Tyler's disappearance she had started to get excited about being a professional surfer. But she would give it all up in the click of a finger to have her brother back home.

Jaspa shivers, and slips her feet underneath the sheet. 'Hey, I saw you pulling Cooper aside at Kamas. What were you talking about?' She can't believe she's even brought it up.

'Oh, errr,' Mel stumbles. 'Nothing too important. I was just grilling him about getting everyone he knows to help look for Tyler.' She chews her lip as Anthony pokes his head through the door, his timing impeccable.

'Honey, your mum and I are going to bed. We're not hungry – can you fix yourself something?'

'Sure, Dad,' Jaspa says through a yawn. 'How's Mum doing?'

They had arrived home from the search to find Ellen in Tyler's room, lying on his bed staring at the wall. Anthony had gestured to the girls to give them some time alone, so Jaspa and Mel had flopped on Jaspa's bed and snoozed.

'Not too good, she needs some sleep. They'll resume the search in the morning.' He walks to the bed, bends down and holds Jaspa's head with one hand, drawing it against his lips. 'Good night, button. Love you,' he says with a quiver in his voice.

'Love you to Venus and back,' she replies to the closing door, feeling like a kid again. They used to play with terms of affection when she was younger; thinking up faraway places to mark the enormity of their love.

'Are you hungry? I'm not hungry.' Jaspa gets up and fishes out a pale blue T-shirt from her laundry basket. She gives it a sniff and deems it acceptable for one more wear.

'No, not yet. Do you want me to crash here with you tonight, or would you rather some alone time? Either way, I'd better let Mum know.' Mel scoops up her phone from the bedside table.

'Please stay, it's a good distraction.' Jaspa walks to her sliding doors and opens them to greet the cooler night air. The moon, almost full, beams onto the ocean, glistening with the movement of each wave. How could something that brings her such joy be the cause of such pain?

Mel joins her, leaning on the railing and drawing in a deep breath of salty oxygen.

'The wind's dropped right off, and the swell's about

half the size it was this morning. That's a good thing, right?' Jaspa asks, digging deep for optimism.

'That's a great thing,' Mel comforts, giving her a slight nudge with her elbow.

'Do you want to go to bed yet? I'm not sure if I'll even be able to sleep after our nanna nap.' Jaspa flops against the railing like a towel hung out to dry.

Mel walks back inside, over to Jaspa's antique dressing table, and checks her skin for blackheads. 'Nah, I'm not tired yet, either,' she says, attempting to excavate one from its crater. 'But there is something I reckon we should do.'

'What?' Jaspa questions dubiously, suddenly exhausted at the thought of a Mel adventure.

'Well, what's that saying you always have about the universe, like when crappy things happen?' Mel asks, rubbing her chin with a tissue.

Jaspa turns to face Mel and closes her eyes. 'That when the sea of life is rough, to ride through it knowing it's this way for a reason, that the next journey or lesson is on the horizon, even if you can't see it yet. Trust the universe, basically.' She opens her eyes and jumps onto the bed, hugging her pillow. 'I didn't make it up, though. I kinda adapted it from Buddhism. Why?'

'I reckon we should sit on the beach and send out some positive vibes to Tyler and the universe, almost like praying.'

'Melissa Appleby, are you suggesting we *meditate*? I

never thought I'd see the day ...' Jaspa teases, not forgetting the number of times Mel has taunted her for her interest in 'hippy crap'.

'Yeah, yeah, I know. Just don't go buying me sandal-wood-scented tie-dyed fisherman's pants for Christmas, okay?'

#30

Tyler's not sure how long the blue swimmer crab has been crawling on his collarbone, but he vaguely remembers dreaming about being tickled. He was weight training at school, finally nailing a 100-kilogram lift, when a 5-inch tall elf-like man started tickling him with a feather, challenging Tyler to focus his energy on his weightlifting task and not be consumed by the distraction. The mini-man repeatedly told Tyler this would be the biggest obstacle in his life; to stay in the present moment rather than allowing his mind to stray and obsess over the things he can't control. The more he focused on the weights and ignored the feather, the lighter the lift became. Soon he had no awareness of a feather, or an elf-man, or anything at all other than the bar above his head, and he'd never felt more proud of himself than in that moment.

He instinctively brushes the crab away before opening his eyes to see it scramble like a ballerina towards the rock cave behind him. It takes a few seconds for him to register where he is, and the situation he is in.

The ocean is still lapping against the rock he is using as shelter, but its viciousness has calmed, like a rabid dog finally laid to rest. He chews on a bit of the kelp he used as a pillow last night. He's not sure if it's a good thing to do, but at least it's *something* to do.

Tyler has thought a lot about his sister over the past twenty-four hours, even before he jumped off the Kamikazes ledge. He doesn't enjoy being an asshole, it's just become habitual. It's like he can't be nice anymore, because that would require admitting his meanness. Is he jealous of Jaspa because surfing comes so easily to her? Or because she's got the potential to be the best? Maybe it's because she doesn't think about any of that, she just surfs for the love of it. All of the above, probably. He promises himself that if he finds his way home he'll lay right off and appreciate his sister for who she is – sweet, vague, gangly, light-hearted and accepting.

He rolls onto his stomach to give his back a break from the rocky surface. His throbbing ankle just feels like it's part of him now. As do the weakness, migraine, stinging skin, sea mite bites, sleepiness, open wounds and the desire to drink a swimming pool's worth of fluids. The rising sun melts away the goosebumps that have covered him thanks to a night submerged in water.

Tyler hears a humming noise and a whoosh of water coming from the south. He grits his teeth and props himself up on his elbows to concentrate on the approaching sounds. After what he can only assume is an engine cuts out, male voices can be heard laughing and talking over each other. He guesses there are three, maybe even four of them – he hears several bodies splash into the ocean. He can't see them, but they can't be more than 50 metres away, just around the corner of the headland. Tyler assumes they must be diving for lobster, which are in abundance along this stretch of coastline.

Tyler is giddy with the realisation that this, right now, may be his only chance of being rescued. Two choices present themselves clearly in his mind. He needs to muster every ounce of energy he has left and either drag himself out onto the rock ledge as far as he can and hope the search party returns and sees him, or get himself to that boat. The rock route around the headland is unmanageable on foot, even for someone without his injuries, so the only option is to swim. Will he get one stroke in and collapse? Will he even make it into the ocean without getting smashed against the rocks?

This could be the second dumbest decision he's ever made …

#31

Jaspa looks oddly at her phone. Carolyn has just texted her to say she's at the front door, which is something she's never done in their five-year friendship. Knowing what to say and how to act when someone you care about is in crisis is one of life's greatest challenges. Do you say sorry? Do you try to take their mind off things? Do you simply sit in silence?

'Hey,' Carolyn offers softly as Jaspa opens the door.

Jaspa's blue eyes have lightning bolts of red striking through them, and they're strained with sadness. That morning, as the tip of the sun crept onto the horizon, Jaspa, Anthony, Ellen and Mel joined the search at Pebble Cove, one beach north of Shellhaven. Seeing her mother wade into the water, fully clothed and repeatedly screeching Tyler's name, was too much. A crushing feeling had pressed in on Jaspa's chest, her head swirling like a spinning top. She'd bolted behind a cluster of rocks and fallen to her knees on the sand. Finally alone, she'd let her body go limp, at last allowing herself to be overwhelmed as tears flooded her eyes long before the sobs had time to catch up.

'Thanks for coming,' Jaspa says, bending down to give Carolyn a hug and guiding her through the door.

A darkness weighs heavy in the air, a rarity at 1 Ocean View Avenue. Ellen is lying on the couch talking on the phone, while Anthony sits beside her, rubbing the arches of her feet with one hand and typing into his laptop with the other.

Jaspa and Carolyn walk over to join Mel at the marble breakfast bar, lifting themselves onto the two spare stools. 'Mum's just on the phone to one of the officers. Sounds like they're going to widen the search now the swell has dropped,' Jaspa says, leaning on her elbows. 'It's weird, I *know* he's okay. Like, I'm aware that sounds crazy, but I *know* it. I feel it in my bones.'

Mel and Carolyn smile and nod, trying to support her optimism.

'Tell Carolyn about Cooper,' Mel says to Jaspa, grasping for a subject change to break the silence. Carolyn stares with an open-mouthed smirk at Mel, then turns towards Jaspa without changing her expression.

Jaspa puffs out a snort, her eyes still downcast. 'Oh, he just sent a text to make sure me and Mum and Dad are okay, and apologised for being a weirdo that day on the beach. That's about it, but it was nice to hear from him.'

While Jaspa's head is down, Carolyn mouths to Mel, 'Have you told?' and discreetly nods at Jaspa.

Mel shakes her head furiously, wide-eyed. Now's not the time to pile upon Jaspa's mound of emotion. Carolyn tucks her foot underneath her. 'You know, just an FYI, I drove past the point on the way here and it's really starting to clean up,' she trails off, leaving the comment open-ended.

'Okay, back up there for a minute, sunshine,' Mel says, rolling her index fingers around each other in the air. 'What exactly do you mean, *drove*?'

'Ha, well, Mum was being lame so I just figured I'd borrow her wheels for a while. No biggie,' Carolyn shrugs. The fact that she's not even on her learner's is a minor detail, easily overcome with fake P plates, super cautious driving and a little prayer to whoever is listening.

A trace of a smile plays over Jaspa's lips, which feels much nicer than the southerly direction they've been plummeting in for the past twenty-four hours. She's decided that until there's any evidence that suggests otherwise, she's going to muster as much positivity as possible and hope that it rubs off on her parents. 'You're so much more badass than me. Were you worried about the police?' Jaspa asks Carolyn.

'Yeah, of course, a little, but I just tried not to do anything suss that would make them want to pull me over. I had to come and see you guys, this is too important.'

Jaspa wraps her arms around Carolyn's shoulders and plants an exaggerated kiss in her hair. 'Naw, thanks so much for breaking the law for me – just don't do it again!'

Jaspa loves the idea of going for a quick surf at the point. It's been at least a month since it's been pumping. 'Dad,' she asks softly, towards the living room, 'do you know what time we're heading out to search again? Do we have time for a paddle?' She begins to feel a sense of urgency, suddenly realising how much she's missed the ocean, craving the salty taste around her lips.

Anthony leans on the arm of the couch and turns to face the kitchen. 'Yes, you girls hit the waves for a while. The police are scouring every bit of the coast, so there's not much more we can do at the moment.' He adjusts his laptop and continues to type. 'Oh, and get a couple for me while you're out there, will you?' He winks.

Jaspa, Mel and Carolyn tuck their surfboards under their arms and stride down the driveway to see playful overhead waves pushing from the rocky point all the way into the bay, offering a wall of water to dance on for at least 100 metres.

Jaspa sighs to herself. Surfing: the ultimate distraction to wash away anything that might be on the mind, no matter how awful.

* * *

If a freak set comes, Tyler is a goner. The moment he pulled himself along the rocks and hoisted his body into the ocean, he made a commitment he couldn't sidle away from. He clutches onto a shelf of reef. The small empty fishing boat is now only 15 metres away. If his body could be diagrammed to show the pain he feels, he would be shaded in red from head to toe. There have been moments in the past twelve hours where he almost wished death would scoop him up and do what had to be done. But now he's seen a ray of light breaking through the darkness, urging him to grit his teeth and fight for his life. A worthwhile life, he realises.

The air travels from his nose down into the depths of his belly like a wind tunnel. It's an exercise he learnt during a free-diving lesson at school, to assist with the less enjoyable part of surfing: the hold-down. That moment when a wave slams on top of you, shoving your body towards the bottom, then pins you there like a game that's gone too far. Now, Tyler's using this breathing technique not only to fill himself with as much oxygen as he can, but to also calm his nerves.

On his final inhale, he pushes from the rock with his feet and manages two strokes of freestyle before realising there's no way he has enough stamina for that. He reverts to dogpaddling, arching his head back to keep the water out of his mouth. The mid-afternoon sun pierces through the wisps of cloud, scorching the side of his face. It's like putting a burnt pie back into the oven on high. The undercurrent and lapping swell seesaws him from side to side.

While struggling to stay afloat he sees something. He only gets a glimpse – it's about five metres to his right, and it's big. Anxiety pounds his ribcage. There's no way he can take on a shark right now. Would fate really be that cruel? A figure pierces through the water. Tyler releases a yelp, though his exhausted body barely shudders.

'Holy eff! Dudes, it's Tyler!' The young man rips off his snorkelling mask, swims to Tyler and flips him into an ocean rescue position, then starts stroking towards the boat. He yells for his friends to surface and they help pull him up on board. Tyler can hear muffled voices around him, shouting for someone to ring the cops, and to chase after the rescue ski they spotted earlier. Tyler curls up in a ball on the deck and sobs a tearless cry.

* * *

This is hands-down the best surf session of the year. The wind has dropped off to a very light offshore, so what previously looked like mounds of mashed potato in the ocean are now perfectly formed waves. Jaspa paddles back towards Mel and Carolyn after her fifth multi-turn ride, looking at the crystals of sunlight bouncing off the ocean. Is it possible to be super happy and super sad at the same time? She spots her dad in the line-up and guesses he must need to wash away his helplessness, too. As she gets closer she realises he seems to be … smiling.

'What's going on?' Jaspa asks as she reaches three faces beaming at her, their mouths grinning wider than the length of her last ride.

'Button, they found him. Tyler's been found. We have to go – they're taking him to the hospital.'

Jaspa can't compute the words. They bounce about in her head and for a few moments she's eerily calm, before being flooded with a sense of relief.

She paddles over to Anthony, leaning her torso partway across his board and drawing her arms around his shoulders. 'Oh, Dad, that's the best. Is he okay? How did they find him?' Before he can answer, a set of swell swoops in towards them and Jaspa yells, 'Party wave!'

All four surfers turn their boards at the same time and take the drop together. Jaspa cuts back and soars underneath Mel and Carolyn, then transitions to whip her board back around in front of Anthony. They continue to loop in and out of one another's manoeuvres, offering high-fives, stomping their back feet to produce sprays in each other's faces, and seeing who can race down the line the fastest. Just as they near the shore of the bay, Jaspa positions herself above her dad, rips off her leg-rope and hops onto his board, leaving hers to be carried in by the whitewater. She holds onto his boardshorts and rides tandem, just like they used to when she was little. They soar along the unbroken section, timing their movements perfectly, bobbing up and down to create speed. Just as a closeout section threatens to munch them into its sandy jaws, Jaspa leaps into the air in a starfish pose, screaming, 'Thanks for the lift, Dad!' and belly flops over the back of the wave.

     #32

'Move it up about half an inch, honey.' Grandma Ryder
is lying on the couch, feet crossed, looking over her
reading glasses, the newspaper crossword puzzle resting
on her lap. Today she's rocking a pink and gold past-
the-knee kaftan, and her silver spikey bob is coated with
hair gel.

'How's this?' Jaspa asks, having repositioned the
'Welcome Home Tyler!' sign she's made out of shells,
seaweed, and sand coloured with food dye, all stuck to a
strip of calico. Grandma holds up two thumbs, then
rests her head back against the cushion.

Jaspa presses the sign into place, then takes a step
down to admire her work. It's still skewed a bit too far
to the right – enough to make Mel cringe, but Jaspa
barely notices.

'When will they be home from the doc, Mum?'

Jaspa asks, climbing down from the stepladder. Her brother was discharged from hospital ten days ago, but has been mostly bed-bound since. Jaspa has spent almost every moment by his side, trying not to feel partially responsible – and perhaps overdoing the nurturing. Tyler had to ask her to chill and allow him some alone time to mend his mind. To recount all the moments of jealousy and anger that had possessed him over the past two years, recognise them for what they were, then attempt to piece it all together and work out how to be a better human.

Ellen brushes out the bumps in the tablecloth. 'They'll be home any minute, it was just a quick check-up. Here, love,' she says, handing Jaspa two platters of food. 'Everything that's on this bench, plus the pastries in the oven, need to go out.'

'Yum scrum pastries. Tyler's favourite?'

'Of course! By special request, in fact,' Ellen says, moving a pile of magazines from the bench into the rack.

'Mum, when's Tyler's article going to be out?' Jaspa has been eagerly waiting for the latest edition of *Soul Reviver*. Of the six magazines that approached Tyler for an interview, he chose the one known for its in-depth articles and beautiful imagery, and was further coaxed by their promise to use award-winning surf journalist Sean Baker. Sean spoke at length to Tyler about the pressures of pursuing a competitive surfing career, sharing the spotlight with his sister, not dealing well with losses, getting a grip on anxiety, along with a gut-wrenching description of his experience from the moment he descended the Kamikazes headland to his rescue.

'It should be out next week, honey. Sean is going to hand deliver a copy as soon as it's printed,' Ellen says, pouring a mango juice for her mother-in-law and taking it to her.

Jaspa hears car doors slamming outside. 'Yay, they're here! Let me know if there's anything else I need to do, Mum.' She waits, grinning widely at the front door, eager for Tyler to see all of the effort she's put into his party. Apart from Cooper, Tyler hasn't felt up to seeing any of his friends since the rescue. When first approaching consciousness in the hospital bed, he admitted to Jaspa that he'd been grappling with two main feelings: guilt and embarrassment. His story had been splashed over every corner of the media, and although the primary concern was for his safe return, the writers couldn't help but speculate on the inner workings of his mind, something he hadn't figured out either. But now Tyler is ready to celebrate with the friends and family who consumed his thoughts during those twenty-eight hours of hell, which he's now grateful for every second of.

'Whoa, this looks sick as.' Tyler hobbles through the door on crutches, taking in the homemade welcome sign, the bunting of cut-out surfing images and the table laden with food. 'Can I help with anything?'

'Nup, I think we're just about done, aren't we, Mum?' Jaspa beams, jiggling up and down on her toes excitedly.

'Yes, love. Dad will just fill the bathtub with ice. Everyone should be here soon. Are you feeling okay?' Ellen asks from around the fridge door.

'Yeah, Mum, I'm good. Bit grogged from the meds, but pretty pumped about finally seeing everyone and telling them about our plans for next year,' he says, giving his sister a wink.

'Just call us the dream team!' Jaspa looks up to see Mel and Carolyn at the door and screams in delight.

'Rumour has it there's a pumping party to be had,' Mel sings as she dances through the door then throws her arms around Tyler – probably a tad too tightly, given what his body has been through.

Tyler laughs and cringes away from her rib tickles. 'Thanks for coming, girls. It's great to see you, even if you are totally annoying, Mel Appleby.'

'You're looking really well, man, stoked to have you back,' Carolyn pipes in, while eyeing off the table of treats, trying to decide what she's going to shove in her mouth first.

Tyler opens Spotify on his phone and selects his 'mad tunes' playlist, with Kendrick Lamar the first to soar through the surround sound speakers, just as a bunch of his friends arrive carrying a cardboard box full of PS3 games.

'This'll keep you occupied while we're out catching your waves, buddy,' Cooper says, mocking Tyler about the four weeks he has to wait before he can surf again. The guys encircle Tyler in a back-slapping embrace.

'Okay, you lunatics, let me outta the ring of bromance for a second. I've got an important announcement. Jaspa, come 'ere, it's time.' Tyler gestures for Jaspa to stand next to him.

'Firstly, I want to thank my little sister for being just the nicest person I know. And I want to congratulate her on making the tour.' Tyler bends his head close to Jaspa's ear and whispers, 'You tell them, you should be the one to tell them.'

Jaspa's cheeks flush and her stomach chucks a back-flip. She hasn't even told her best friends yet – now she has to tell a room full of his eager-faced mates? 'Well …' she begins, avoiding Cooper's eyes, but catching Mel and Carolyn's puzzled look. 'Tyler *is* in fact coming on tour next year … as my coach!' She leans into Tyler's side as he rests his arm on her shoulder.

'Yep, it's true, dudes. In between earning coin at the chicken shop and trying to qualify again through the local comps, I'm going to travel as Jaspa's chaperone and help her win that junior world title.'

As Tyler's friends talk over each other, cheering excitedly, Jaspa shrugs and grins at Mel, whose mouth is open like a feeding fish. 'Let's eat before the boys scoff it all,' Jaspa suggests, coaxing Mel and Carolyn towards the table.

'Wow, that's some news,' Mel says, once they've loaded their plates and escaped to the front porch daybed.

'I know, right? I'm really excited for him. Mum and Dad say it'll give Tyler a sense of purpose.' Jaspa was as surprised as anyone when Tyler approached her with the idea, but while he was missing she vowed to do whatever it took to keep him from doing something stupid again, and she plans to keep her promise.

'Don't get me wrong, I'm all for it,' Mel says, mopping up a glob of hummus with a carrot stick. 'As long as your best interest is his.'

'All I really care about is that he's safe and happy and acting normal again,' Jaspa says. 'Anyway, we *all* get someone to watch over us now.' She knows there will be ups and downs with her brother joining her journey, but having him alive and in her life is worth any bit of annoyance he might throw her way.

'Yo,' Carolyn pipes in, intercepting any judgment Mel might be about to spit back at Jaspa, 'did ya see all the props The Bikini Collective page is getting? Girls are frothin' over it!'

'I did!' Mel mumbles around a mouthful of food before gulping it down. 'And I thought your post on both loving and fearing the ocean was stunning,' she says to Jaspa before releasing a thunderous burp.

Jaspa turns and waves her hand in front of her mouth. 'Oh, ewww, you're foul. That reeks of garlic!' She's grinning though, thrilled that Mel likes her story. The ocean is full of contradictions, and after what Jaspa has been through the past month the words poured from her like an incoming tide. 'I'd like to upload more entries if that's okay with you two?'

'For surezy,' Mel says, wiping the plate with her finger then licking it. 'There's also a bunch of questions posted this week that we should probably answer.'

'I'll help with that,' Jaspa jumps in. 'They're so cute! Did you see the one asking how to convince your parents to drive you to the beach?' As Jaspa rattles off her top five bribing tips, she notices that Mel is looking through the window, not listening to a word. Eager to see what's so distracting, Jaspa is gobsmacked when she turns to see that Mel's eyes are locked with Cooper's. And then he gives her a subtle nod.

What the heck?

#33

'Jazz, I've gotta tell you something,' Mel says suddenly, grabbing Jaspa's hand.

Jaspa puts down her fork, still speared with pumpkin and spinach salad. Her blood boils, then turns cold. She knows what this means – it's so obvious. Cooper and Mel are in love, and she's going to have to graciously accept that. But then why is Mel smirking at her? Surely she's not so ruthless that she'd break her heart with a laugh?

'What? What? You're freaking me out!' Jaspa croaks, jiggling Mel's hand up and down, trying to shake the truth out of her.

'Well, it turns out you weren't delusional at all in thinking Cooper likes you ...' Mel trails off in a tease.

Jaspa fights the urge to swing back around and look at Cooper. 'And how would you know that?' she asks, playfully but suspiciously, wondering if her best friend has undertaken some kind of psychological torture to make him cave. Trying to hide anything from Mel is as futile as trying to hide food from a fox.

'He told me! It was all his doing, I *swear*!' she laughs, immediately picking up on the subtle accusation. 'On the cliff during the search, he 'fessed up that he's super into you, has been for ages, but Tyler warned you were totes off limits.' Mel puts her plate down, then hoists her knee up on the couch, wriggling closer to Jaspa. 'That's half of what their fight was about at the Rocket Fuel party.'

'Don't look now, but Cooper is fully gawking straight at you, *and* talking to Tyler,' Carolyn informs Jaspa, a chicken leg in hand.

'Right then, it's time, come on.' Mel jumps to her feet and offers – not that she'd accept a refusal – her hand, pulling Jaspa up to join her.

Jaspa freezes in place, shifting all her weight to her bum in an attempt to remain sitting safely here, where there's no risk of having rejection spear through her heart again.

Mel uses two hands to clench Jaspa's wrists. 'I will use force if necessary.' She leans back and wrenches her friend to her feet, then affectionately cups her hands over Jaspa's. 'I know you're freaked, but remember that all of our most exhilarating, adrenaline-filled experiences have started out with a bit of fear. Think of this as being like the moment you finally get to surf Hawaii – scary, but worth it. Am I right?'

Jaspa relaxes her hands into Mel's and smiles nervously. 'Okay. But please, please, don't let me wipe out. Promise?'

'I promise.'

Jaspa's heartbeat bounces to the doof tune that's playing, and her cheeks ripen as though they've been pinched a dozen times. She follows Mel to the crowd of guys, each step seemingly taking a hundred seconds longer than it should. Mel shows no mercy, leading Jaspa straight to Cooper's side. His face warms immediately, with no trace of the coldness he had shown on the beach that day. Draping an arm around her shoulders, he leans in towards her. 'Jaspa, I'm so glad to see you. Can we talk?' he whispers.

Jaspa gulps, then nods, and they slip away seemingly discreetly, although every eye in the room follows.

Cooper has his index finger entwined with Jaspa's, which is even cuter and more romantic than holding hands. She follows him to the bench at the front of her house that overlooks the point. He flops down to sit and playfully pulls her onto the bench, so her legs drape over his. He strokes his fingers along her shins, and they tingle with his touch.

'Jaspa, I just want to say I'm so incredibly sorry about giving you such mixed messages. At dinner, and then when I saw you at the beach. I was a real asshole.'

'It did upset me, actually. I don't like it when I can't read what someone is thinking. I guess I was mainly embarrassed by it all,' she says through wisps of her wind-blown hair.

He tucks his arm between the bench and her back, drawing her closer. 'I think you are sweet, and amazing, and gobsmackingly gorgeous, and a much better surfer than me,' he laughs. 'And I haven't been able to think about any other girl for the past, maybe, year or more.'

Jaspa feels his breath skimming along her cheekbone and she slowly rubs her lips together to wet them, both as a nervous gesture and perhaps also to prepare them for what she hopes is to come. 'So why were you so weird towards me on the beach that day?' she asks softly, the hurt flashing in her eyes.

He hangs his head. 'It's … it's kinda complicated. Don't get mad at him, but Tyler just struggled with the thought of his best mate dating his sister. I guess it's understandable.'

'To be honest, I'm not that surprised. Before he went missing he'd been pretty awful to me.' She squints into the sun and rubs her dress fabric between her thumb and forefinger. 'I just tried to ignore it and put it down to hormones. He's worse than a girl!' she says, shaking her head.

Cooper laughs, exposing his dimple. Jaspa's so tempted to touch it. 'You know, Jaspa, it's probably got way more to do with your surfing. It's no coincidence he started wigging out when you started getting so good and everyone began paying attention, even if you didn't realise it. He's jealous, which sucks for him because he's really talented, too. He's just got lots of stuff he needs to work on if he wants to be the best. But you, you could almost click your fingers and be there, if you wanted to.'

Jaspa doesn't know why people keep telling her this. She's only fifteen, and only just made the tour. Can't she just enjoy that for a while without being told she could be the best? She politely bats away the compliment.

'Oh, I don't know about that. I just want to have fun and support my friends, travel the world and see what happens. Most importantly, I want to always be in love with surfing. I love it so much.'

Cooper takes this moment to rest his other hand on her cheek, fixing his eyes on hers. 'Jaspa, I think, no, I *know*, I will always be in love with *you*.'

Before Jaspa has a chance to respond, he presses his lips onto hers, lingering there for several seconds without moving, then slowly deepens the kiss, breaking up the passionate movements with tender pecks on her cheeks. He draws back to meet her gaze, brushing her hair back with his fingers before kissing her again, this time allowing his tongue to gently greet hers, coaxing it to dance inside their mouths. Jaspa feels as though delicious warm caramel has been poured all over her. This is like doing a perfectly timed cutback from the open face back up into the crest of foam, ready to race the wave again. That synchronicity, the adrenaline, the beauty of being so connected. And the fact that he is so damn *yummy*. The best thing about dreams is when they start to come true.

#34

'You did *what?*' Mel gasps down the line.

Jaspa squeezes her phone between her cheek and shoulder to free up her hands. Waving to Cooper as he drives away, Jaspa scoops up her brand-new custom surfboard and jiggles it under her arm. It's a perfect fit. The rails, thin with a subtle upturn, lightly rest behind her knuckles, the texture as smooth as an ocean glass-off, yet to be blemished by wax, dings and zinc stains. 'I, umm, I kinda told him I love him,' Jaspa replies with a giggle.

'Whoa. When? Where? How? Spill. Now.'

Jaspa leans against the front door, rummaging through her faux leather embroidered handbag for her house keys. 'Well, we were out surfing and he let me have the wave of the day, so I screamed, "Thank you, I love you!"'

It wasn't until Jaspa was paddling back out that she realised what she'd said. Did that count as an official declaration? She isn't sure; she's never said it to a boyfriend before.

'Hmmm,' Mel croaks into the phone. 'Giving away set waves *is* almost love-worthy in my eyes. If he also lends you his boards, this dude's a keeper.'

'Actually, he's done better than that.' Jaspa flips her board to fit vertically through the door. 'He introduced me to his shaper and I'm now on the team with him and Trudy Hardwick!'

'What the? You're getting sticks from Darren Hanson? That guy's a genius, he could make an ironing board rippable.'

'I know, I had to pinch myself. I just this minute picked up my board and it feels divine.' Jaspa pushes the door open to see Tyler asleep on the couch. 'Hey, I've gotta go,' she whispers. 'I'll come over later to surf.'

'Okay, I'd better go too before I vomit jealousy down the phone. And don't for a second think I'm not going to snag a few waves on your new ride. Love you.'

'Love you back. Bye.' Jaspa closes the door behind her and rests her board on the rug as Tyler stirs, looking blearily at Jaspa through half-slit eyes.

'Hey, Tyler, I got your text so came straight home. How are you feeling?' She walks to the kitchen to pour two glasses of coconut water.

'I'm okay. It's been a bit of a weird day, and the

tablets still make me feel a bit rank.' Tyler sits up so Jaspa can flop down beside him.

She hands him his drink and he takes a sip, the cracks disappearing as his lips rub together.

'You sure you're all good?' she asks with eyebrows raised. Her brother looks like he's got a million things on his mind.

'Actually,' he says with a chuckle to himself, 'I'm *really* fricken good. I've got something to show you.' He reaches towards the floor and fumbles about, trying to find his phone. Picking it up and tapping into his Gmail account, he opens up an email and hands it to Jaspa, whose mouth falls wide open as she reads a message from the director of the tour's Australian division.

Tyler, we're incredibly sorry to hear what happened to you and hope you're well on your way to recovery. All of us here send our regards. I'm writing to inform you that Daniel Larkin has had to step down from his position on the tour due to family concerns. You are next in the rankings to join the team on the world tour, if you choose to accept. Please kindly inform us of your decision by 2 January, and don't hesitate to contact us with any queries. We hope to have you on board.

'Wow, Tyler I can't believe it,' is all Jaspa can manage. Just when she thought everything was sorted, life sends another closeout set to try and get under.

She's ecstatic for her older brother, but also worried he'll revert back to his old attitude. And does this mean he won't be her support on the tour? She got so used to the idea, she's not sure if she can do it without him now – or with him in competition mode. His little sister will be the last thing on his agenda.

She pauses a moment and looks into Tyler's eyes, which are glistening with a mix of excitement and fear. No matter what, she has bucketloads of love for her brother and will support whatever path he takes. She leans across and hugs him with one arm. 'I'm so happy for you, it's turned out exactly as it's meant to be.' She sits back, staring at the email. 'So, have you made a decision?'

Tyler nods slowly. Taking back the phone, he types in a reply, then looks up at Jaspa. 'I reckon this is the best thing for both of us.' He hesitates for a few seconds, then presses send.

Your surf speak glossary!

a-frame a wave peak that peels both left and right.

backside/backhand riding a wave with your back to the ocean.

backdoor entering a barrel from behind the peak.

backwash when water pushes from the shore back towards a regular breaking wave, causing them to collide.

barrel/tube the hollow part of a breaking wave, which surfers can ride inside of, completely hidden from a shore view.

beach break waves that break over sand.

bottom turn generally the first turn you do, performed at the bottom of the wave.

closeout a wave that shuts down without peeling left or right.

cutback a turn you do on the open face to position yourself back near the critical pocket of the wave.

deck the side of the surfboard you lie down on.

drop the ride when you take off on a wave with the pitching lip.

duckdive pushing your board underneath a breaking a wave so you can pop out the other side.

face the 'green' smooth part of a breaking wave that isn't the whitewater.

floater a manoeuvre that involves gliding over the

whitewater, usually so you can reach the open face or finish a ride.

frontside/forehand riding a wave facing the ocean.

glassy/glass-off when there is little to no wind and the ocean is smooth like a mirror.

goofy footer a surfer who stands on a board with their right foot forward. (The same term is also used for skateboarding and snowboarding.)

grommet/grom a young kid who surfs.

Huey the surfing god.

impact zone a spot in the line-up where the waves are breaking with the most power (don't get caught there!).

inside the position that's closest to the breaking pocket of the wave, where you have priority to take off over any other surfer. (The term 'caught on the inside' is also used when you're stuck in the impact zone.)

interference when a competitor drops in or obstructs the path of the surfer who has right of wave. The penalty is usually removal of the interferer's highest score.

kook/gumby a derogatory term used to describe someone who isn't a very good surfer.

layback a forehand manoeuvre where you end a turn by laying your back close to the water. A very '70s-style move.

left-hander a wave that peels left from the viewpoint of the surfer on the wave.

leg-rope the leash that attaches to your surfboard, which is wrapped around the ankle on your back leg.

line-up a position in the ocean where waves are breaking and the surfers are sitting.

lip the first point of a wave that pitches over. The lip can vary in intensity, from throwing with force to form a barrel, to crumbling along the face.

lull the time between sets when no waves are breaking.

natural footer a surfer who stands on a board with their left foot forward. (The same term is also used for skateboarding and snowboarding.)

offshore wind a wind blowing from the land onto the water, which makes the ocean nice and smooth.

ollie getting air by hopping the front of the board out of the water.

onshore wind a wind blowing from the ocean onto the land, making the ocean bumpy and sometimes tricky to surf.

outside a position that's on the other side of the surfer who's closest to the breaking pocket of the wave. When you're there you have to give way to the inside surfer, unless they encourage you to 'GO!'

out the back the furthest out to sea you can be, on the other side of the breaking whitewater, while still in a position to catch waves.

overhead when you're riding a wave and its face is taller than you are.

over the falls when you take off but don't get to your feet, and fall with the pitching lip. Wipeout!

peak the point of a wave that pitches up, ready to break.

pop-up jumping to your feet on the take-off – the quicker, the better!

pull in what you do when you see a tube/barrel forming before you.

quiver collective noun for surfboards.

rail the edges around the sides of a surfboard, which you ideally want to carve deep into the water on your turns.

reef break a wave that breaks over reef – sometimes dead coral, sometimes alive. Be careful of your feet!

right-hander a wave that peels right from the view-point of the surfer on the wave.

roundtail when the tail of a surfboard is rounded – often preferred for barrelling waves.

re-entry (reo) a manoeuvre where you soar vertically into the top pocket of the wave and snap the board around underneath you.

set a group of waves that are usually bigger than the average on the day.

shaper someone who makes surfboards.

soul arch when you're on a wave and you stand styl-ishly still and tall for a moment with your back arched, old-school style!

squaretail when the tail of a surfboard is squared off at the end.

swallowtail a v-shape cut out of the tail of a surfboard.

take-off the moment you stop paddling for a wave and stand on your surfboard.

wipeout ooops, you've fallen off the wave!

The
Bikini
Collective
Book 2: Lost in LA
by Kate McMahon

Pack your bags, the Bikini Collective girls are California bound to compete in their very first overseas surfing event. The LA sun is shining, Santa Monica's shops are bursting with bargains and the point break is pumping. It should be happy days, right? Wrong! Mel has her party pants on and is ready to ravage this Hollywood scene, but her best friend and wingwoman, Jaspa, is welded to the hip of her new boyfriend. If Jaspa wants to be the Mayor of Lame Town, Mel figures she'll just have to find someone else to get into trouble with. Swept along by the local celebrity brat pack, Mel finds herself on a wild ride that soon lands her in deep water. This is an adventure to rival any rogue set, so hold your breath and dive down deep … and pray you pop back up again!

"A ride so fun and wild, I wanted to stowaway in their surfboard bags."
Laura Enever

"An exhilarating read that beautifully captures the spirit of being a young professional surfer growing up on tour, and the complicated dynamics of competing against best friends." **Jessi Miley-Dyer**

The
Bikini
Collective
Book 3: Sea of Gratitude
by Kate McMahon

Book three in *the Bikini Collective* series sees the girls preparing for another action-packed surfing adventure, but one of them is burdened with secrets. With all of her scholarship funds exhausted, Carolyn has no choice: she'll have to drop off the World Junior Tour. Just as all seems lost, the Bikini Collective – along with a mysterious donor – save the day. Next stop: Brazil!

The lush South American tropics are dreamy; playful waves, everyday fiestas and beautiful, smooth-talking Brazilians. But can Carolyn find what it means to truly be happy? Just like a calm ocean with a deceiving undercurrent, things aren't always what they seem.

"McMahon picks you up and drops you into the ocean with her."

Stephanie Gilmore

"Inspiring. Blue Crush *for a new generation."* **Sean Doherty**